BLACKHEATH

AN ELATHIEN SOLO MYSTERY
·
A Novel of the Endlands

I0557681

by
Quinn Hamilton
and
Scott Fitzgerald Gray

Cover, Design, and Typography
by (studio)Effigy

Published by Insane Angel Studios
insaneangel.com

Chapter One — 1

Chapter Two — 6

Chapter Three — 16

Chapter Four — 25

Chapter Five — 35

Chapter Six — 42

Chapter Seven — 50

Chapter Eight — 61

Chapter Nine — 72

Chapter Ten — 82

Chapter Eleven — 93

Chapter Twelve — 100

Chapter Thirteen — 107

Chapter Fourteen — 113

Chapter Fifteen — 122

For Louise

*whose love of reading and mysteries lives on
in her children and grandchildren*

For Béatrice

*When I recall that nevermore, alas!
That lady shall I see
On whose account I mourn with such dismay,
My grieving thoughts about my heart amass
Such sorrow that I say:
"My soul, why dost thou not depart from me...?"*

— ONE —

AGAINST THE SOMBER SILENCE, the cracked black gemstone pulsed with a shrill tone that filtered only into the hearing of the one who carried it. The sound of its summons was a thing that Magister Sirnos had long grown used to. He smoothed the seam of his black robe as he slipped a hand to its outside pocket. Then with a finger's touch on the gem, a voice was in his mind, issuing distant commands that only he could hear.

He responded to those commands in the same manner that they came to him — through focused thought that left no chance of being overheard. The wary darkness of his expression told of the importance of this silent conversation. The implacable evenness of his voice in his own mind told of how aware Sirnos was that the mind at the other end of the gemstone's spell could sense his agitation.

One hand futilely squeezed the black gem as that other mind unfolded within his, as if Sirnos might be subconsciously trying to constrain the stone's power. The other hand pressed down on the top of the lacquered black desk beside which the magister stood. Its wood was yewn, thin-grained and imposingly dark. An artifact from an older time, it was quite possibly the most valuable item in an office filled with wonders both magical and mundane. Sirnos had dated its construction at nearly five centuries past, in a time when the great Yewnwood still pushed up to the edges of the Free City itself.

With a terse acknowledgement that the conversation was done, the magister let his finger slip from the gemstone, feeling the link break with the faintest echo. Leaning more heavily on the desk, he stared into the shadows that fell outside the shimmering gleam of an evenlamp, shrouded where it burned bright and cold. Within those shadows, shelves of scrolls and bound volumes lined the walls. Framed parchments hung between them as notes and declarations of guild affiliations, professional accomplishments, and a long list of academic credentials.

Sirnos was an important man. A man of advanced age and great reputation, and far beyond easy subservience to the orders that the voice at the other end of the gemstone's arcane link had tasked him with. But in the end, he knew that he was not as important as the masters of that voice. It was a feeling Sirnos did not enjoy.

The corridor that gleamed white by day was rendered yellow-grey in the night's faint light, the color of old cream. Evenlamps burned at intervals, their haloes shadow-winged by shrouds of heavy night-cloth. The sentry who paced through those shadows was an Ilvani called Tajamynar, a common name among the forest folk. He wore the grey tunic and leggings that was the uniform of the sentries of Blackheath, along with the dark green sash and its silver badge of leaves that was the insignia of the refuge and its healers.

Idly, he flipped through the heavy ring of keys hanging at his belt as he checked the latch at one of the broad stone corridor's many sets of double doors. He worked quietly, pulling to check that the locks were set, then moving on to the next. Each door was marked with a brass plaque hanging on the wall adjacent to its keyhole of black iron. Each plaque was set with a legend, but Tajamynar had long since stopped reading them, just as he had stopped hearing the muted cries of anguish or nightmare that rang out from time to time beyond the doors.

A rattle of other keys heralded the appearance of a figure at the door ahead of him. Her healer's robes flashed white where she passed closest beneath the shrouded light above, fading to grey as she moved on. She nodded gravely to Tajamynar, who turned back to watch her as she passed. He had taken her once, he remembered, in the dark of a locked office in the lower Administration Tower. She had enjoyed it more than he, to judge by her noisy enthusiasm at the time. Still, he appraised the ample sway of her hips now with a thin smile.

Across the corridor, another door opened. Tajamynar heard no telltale rattle of keys, so that as expected, he turned to see the one person who carried no keys in Blackheath. It was the door to the stairs and the northeast Masters' Tower. Standing before it was Sirnos, his black robe fading into the deeper shadow where no light shone behind him.

The magister appraised the young sentry. Tajamynar responded with the briefest nod before he walked away.

Sirnos waited until the sentry's footsteps had faded before he closed the door to the tower stairs. He paced soundlessly along the corridor that the young sentry had just completed his check of, stopping alongside a door like any other. Its brass plaque was well worn, scribed with dark letters to spell out *FEMALE WARD 5th & 3*.

The magister touched his fingers to the door's keyhole, whispering a word to channel arcane force that caused the lock, pins and bolt, to reset itself with barely a click. He pushed the door open. He stepped inside.

Shadow and silence closed in. Dim light welled where a covered evenlamp burned. The space around him had the look of a parlor or sitting room, low chairs and floor cushions scattered about, white-painted tables spread between a dozen narrow doors. A single painting on canvas hung against one patched and plastered wall, a scene of golden fields set with sunflowers.

At the far side of the silent chamber, tall windows showed the light of the city beyond, the sky a dark dome of rushing winter cloud. By bright day, the field of arcane force that protected those windows was invisible to the eye. By dark, however, that magic could be noticed as the faintest ripple of shadow where long fingers of light from outside stretched themselves along the floor.

As the magister walked, his hand slipped into his pocket. Not on the outside of his robe this time, but within it, a cluster of hidden spaces cut of silk and sealed with a dweomer of magic that only his hand could pass. When it emerged, that hand held a sliver of crystal, blood-red in the ward room's dim light.

He paced his way carefully toward the door that was his goal, each of these narrow portals marking the entrance to a cell beyond. All were set with smoothly squared off slates marked with words in white chalk. *Nerani,* this one said — *Dependent of Blackheath* — *Consumption of Faculty and Thought.*

With another whispered word, the cell door unlocked to the touch of Sirnos's hand. He pulled the latch and stepped inside.

The room within was the same grey as the common area beyond it, the same grey as the twisting corridors, the same as any of the identical convalescent wards found on each of Blackheath's uppermost floors. The same shrouded light filled each cell by night, no windows here. No decoration, the whitewashed walls kept clean by minor magic. No furnishings except for a straight-backed chair, the narrow sleeping pallet set along the floor.

Magister Sirnos froze to see that pallet empty.

The rough blankets lay straight and undisturbed despite the lateness of the night. Sirnos turned, scanning the cell reflexively, even though he already knew there was nowhere in the narrow space where the figure he sought could have hidden herself. The door had been locked, no way through it for the convalescent who should have been confined to bed like all the rest of the refuge's residents, sound in a dark slumber.

From behind him, Sirnos heard a shimmering chime, like nails scratching glass. The crystal clutched tight in his fingers flashed as a shiver twisted through his hand.

Through the doorway, the chiming sound rose from the tall window. The magister saw no movement there, but the field of arcane force rippled where its shadow spread across the floor, crosshatch lines vibrating like the strings of a harp.

In the cell with no windows, a storm wind rose. Sirnos staggered back through the open cell door, buffeted by a force that came from nowhere, shrieking in his ears like a stolen scream. He fought to breathe, wind tearing at his robe, choking off his voice even as it failed to so much as touch the chamber around him. Shadowed chairs and cushions showed no sign of its blast, the painting of sunflowers hanging stock still as its edges blackened in Sirnos's vision.

Slowly, the magister's hand forced itself open, jerking as if controlled by some other will. The blood-red crystal twisted from his fingers, swirling airborne as if held on the hands of the wind, even as Sirnos choked and gasped and was drawn within that wind's embrace.

The sentry Tajamynar was descending to the bottom of the central stairs, a great coil of white and black marble whose wide stone steps wound through the center of the topmost four of Blackheath's floors. At each level above, a broad landing was marked by more locked doors, their magical brass bright even in the gloom.

The doors to the second level marked the end of his patrol, beyond which lay the arched mezzanine, closed up and dark for the night. He would hand his keys to the late sentinel there, exchanging word of things heard and unheard as he walked.

By prior arrangement, the presence of the Magister Sirnos on the fifth floor would not be noted with that information.

Tajamynar made the moonsign by instinct, scribing the warding against evil above his heart. He recognized the futility, though, knowing that in the time it had taken him to complete his patrol, the deed would already be done. It wasn't his business to dwell on it.

Even as he approached the doors, through the darkness at the top of the stairs, he heard the strange and sudden hiss of storm wind.

Along the twisting staircase, starting where Tajamynar stepped closer and then coursing upward, a curtain of dust rose. Drawn up the steps, it twisted around and out of sight, carried on higher above by the wind's rising shriek.

The sentry heard the strangled scream as well.

The dark shape fell with a speed that made it impossible to react, made it impossible to look away. Where Sirnos struck the stone railing between the second level and the third, his body shattered unnaturally like some overripe fruit. Head and limbs tore free as his form twisted, slamming the bottom stairs like a sack of blood and bone.

The head bounced with a crack of shattering skull, rolling forward to stop before Tajamynar's feet. The sentry pulled the whistle from his tunic with shaking hands, his heart pounding in his chest as he fought the urge to turn away. He stared at the face for a long moment, assessing the look of terror in Sirnos's wide-open eyes.

When he finally blew the alert, its shrill sound spread through the shadows of the ground floor and was answered almost at once by another. He heard running footsteps, keys in distant doors as the other sentries on guard this night turned out in response to his call.

Magister Sirnos's left arm sprawled in a red-black pool two strides away. As Tajamynar stared, the broken fingers opened, revealing a sharp-edged crystalline shard of black. But even as he watched, the shard crumbled to ash, twisting on the air as it spread silently across the wet shadow of the floor.

— TWO —

IN WINTER, the cold months of Natriss and Bera, no sunlight touched the sunken streets of Mirayth Ward. Set in a low slope of what had once been vale between the river and the southern city walls, its tall tenement blocks shadowed even the brief midday sun that edged above those walls. It was barely dawn now, and a crust of frost lay thick on the stones. By day, it would be smoothed to slick ice by cartwheels and passing feet, then touched by frost again as the early night fell.

Though the end of Bera was approaching, the past two weeks had been cold and clear in the Free City of Yewnyr. Frost streaked the bare-limbed trees of dormant city parks and the glass of windows. Shoals of ice clotted along the edges of the river docks and the gunwales of the southbound boats fresh down the Farwash. This day had dawned even colder and clearer than most, the bright haze of the sky thrusting up beyond the high towers of Hadriembor Ward to the southeast. In that first light, frost-flowers bloomed along the window glass of Blackheath refuge, rising across from the empty street-side patio where Elathien sat.

She watched that icy gleam with unblinking eyes of leaf-green. The tavern behind her was a long while from opening, but she wasn't there for company or custom. The place had been called the Seven Archers when she was here last, but it had changed signs and owners by the look of it. The Seven Winds it was now, just over a year since the last time she had sat near this same spot and stared out at the same view before her.

In all that time, Mirayth had been a ward whose streets she was anxious to avoid — this street before Blackheath most of all.

The wind rose, carrying the scent of piss and ale as it drove a skiff of snow-ice and dead leaves past her feet. Elathien wore her cloak unfurled despite the cold, leaning back against a wall whose grimy windows were as dark as the stones in which they were set. Her hands ignored the chill by virtue of woolen gloves and the fading warmth of a skin of mulled wine she had almost emptied over a long while of waiting. The touch of color at her cheeks spoke less to the cold and more to the quality of the vintage — a heady ten-year-old burgundy from the southlands of Cosiand.

The stark lines of Blackheath's five storeys, its four curved corner towers, the sculpted rose windows were all testament to its origins as a great temple, and marked the structure as old even compared to the high-beamed tenements and stone-walled guildhalls and crafters' shops ranked around it. In full, it was called the Refuge and Healer's Halls of Yewnyr at the Black Heath, named for the once-surrounding farmland that had long since fallen to the Free City's sprawl. The only green still here was the frosted moss that clung to the great building's southern face, yet the memory of that older Black Heath endured. It was synonymous now with the work done behind the walls of the refuge — and the desperate state of the inmates who passed within.

Even this early, traffic was heavy along the street below the great building, Elathien noting the frequency of passing wains and folk on foot, most of them day laborers by their look. Baker's carts and soup-sellers had already taken the best spots along the street side. Latecomers pressing in from the markets farther along the dock wards were jockeying for space between them. However, all of the street traders uniformly avoided Blackheath's angled gate and front walls, abutting the bend of the broad trade way that emptied out to Yanos Street and the docks at Nomn Ward.

The refuge's back sides were flanked by narrow laneways and terraced garden apartments whose best days were long behind them, their vine-strewn walls holding a layer of grime kissed by frost. An imposing structure, the refuge rose as unbuttressed walls that marked the ancient dweomercraft in its construction, its windows arched and narrow, gleaming like cats' eyes.

A significant number of those who passed within Elathien's view were shifting toward her side of the street, she noted. And of those who passed closer to the refuge's grey walls, fully half made the moon-sign as they went. The warding against evil, and against the dark magic that lingered within Blackheath's walls. No one looked up, all of them passing quickly by.

No one, that is, except the figure in the distance. Elathien watched him as he approached. Human or Half-Ilvani by his look. Young, walking at a good clip up from the south as his gaze swept the lines of Blackheath ahead of him. His cloak was the black and red of the Yewnyr Guard, though his insignia was too far away to make out. However, Elathien recognized him as a member of the Guard Investigators even without that badge.

The pace of his step along the stones carried the quickness of a need to be somewhere, even as a careful measure to that step suggested he was in no real hurry to actually arrive. As he walked, his eyes all but ignored the road ahead, scanning to the side, cautious. Always his gaze settling on Blackheath with a detached indifference as he drew closer.

Elathien drained the wineskin with a last pull, stuffing it into the pocket of her cloak. She had been hoping to delay her entrance into Blackheath for a little longer, but her hand had been forced. She didn't know the figure, but she knew that if she let him get too far ahead of her, it would make her job more difficult.

Coming back to Blackheath was going to prove difficult enough, she suspected. She didn't need any additional frustration.

She watched as the figure slipped within the great gates. Then she stood to cross the street and follow.

The gates of Blackheath stood wide as they always did, webbed in frosted shadow. Their openness was a signifier of the refuge's adage that it turned away none who had need of the healers' arts — even those for whom all other aid of magic, alchemy, and herbology had failed. The many for whom the healers of Blackheath were the last and only hope.

Beyond the doors, a broad foyer opened up to rough-cut marble, black and white and grey across the floor. Two healers, hooded and hurrying, passed Elathien without a word as she walked and took in the view around her, an uneasy familiarity in her gaze. The stone-columned mezzanine she stepped into extended to the second floor, the arched and vaulted ceiling rising above her. The architecture within the refuge was ornate. Columns scribed in leaf-vine and woodgrain climbed along walls washed a pristine white, flourishes of the old-city stylings that had been borrowed centuries ago from the Wood-Elves before they and their forest had retreated to the south.

Above her, the railing that flanked the second level's offices and meeting rooms seemed to ripple just slightly. A trick of the evenlamps filling both levels with the light of a bright afternoon, or so a casual glance would suggest. But even without the benefit of detection magic, Elathien could feel the dweomer behind that twisting of the light. A wall of arcane force locked off the ground floor from the levels above, opened only at the stairs and under the eyes of the sentries that stood guard there. A protective barrier that marked the point at which the world outside ended and Blackheath truly began.

Elathien saw the figure in black and red standing to one side of the sentry post at the foot of the stairs, pacing with practiced impatience. He would have sent word of his arrival up to the administrators, and was waiting now for an escort. The efficiency of security in the refuge was a thing Elathien hadn't forgotten.

The investigator gave her no notice as she approached, looking up only as she spoke.

"Good morning and well met," she said. "My name is Elathien. I'll be working with you."

His pale eyes flicked across her even before his head had turned, Elathien reading the young Yewnyr Guard's appraisal of her. She had been told more than once that her face carried a sense of perpetual accusation that put people off, but she herself had never seen it. Her Ilvani blood, on the other hand, stood out more than she liked in the peak of her ears and a pale gleam in the eyes. The former of those features was hidden this morning as it often was. Her auburn hair was rough-cut to her shoulders, her bangs braided with crimson ribbon, the rest left unkempt against any sense of style. She wore a knotted head-scarf that kept it tamed, and which made sure her ears stayed covered — a look familiar to anyone who had ever watched Elathien work.

"I think you have me mistaken for another," the investigator said. He gave a dismissive nod, and a shrug of the shoulders designed to make sure she saw the insignia of the Guard Investigators there in silver thread, the crossed-blades badge of a sergeant above it.

Elathien recognized the edge of bravado in the investigator, taking up her most tactful tone in response. "I assure you, I haven't…"

"I am a sergeant investigator of the Yewnyr Guard," he said curtly, cutting off the explanation Elathien had been set to give him. A faint sheen of pride showed off his newness to that rank, apparently without him knowing it. "I am attending to business of the city. Move along, if you please."

"I was a member of the Guard before your stones dropped, boy, and I'm here on the same business you are." Elathien found herself feeling less tactful suddenly.

In truth, she was barely a dozen summers older than the investigator, but his face changed when he was angry, making him look even younger than he likely was. He was Human for certain at this range. Barely a score of summers behind him, and a thin beard that he had likely been cultivating for a full third of those years. The beard and the hair were dark, but the sky-blue eyes suggested the blood of Norgyr in him somewhere.

"And whose authority exactly brings you here?" he said dismissively.

"Cirhela, Master Healer of Blackheath and member of the Council of Masters. The same one who summoned the Guard last night and begged for a full investigation. Only they sent her you instead. Laicos, is it?"

The young investigator took that in stride. "Knowing Cirhela's name and reading mine off my badge is hardly impressive work. And if you truly did know anything of the Yewnyr Guard, you'd know we work alone."

From inside her sleeve, Elathien produced a bifold leather wallet, flipping it open to reveal her sanctioned investigator's credentials, notarized by the Yewnyr Guard and the Authority of the City Watch. She saw Laicos not bother to hide his contempt. To the members of the professional force that was the Yewnyr Guard, private law enforcement and militias were one step below even the volunteer City Watch forces administered by Yewnyr's individual wards.

"A freelance."

"Called in by Master Cirhela," Elathien said evenly. Alongside her credentials, she produced the silver badge of Blackheath that had come to her shortly before dawn, its interlocking leaves set with ancient healer's runes. Though Laicos had no reason to accept its authenticity, Elathien saw his gaze darken to suggest he did.

From the wallet, she also proffered a printed card. *Elathien,* it said on one line; *Solo* on the next. An address along the bottom was the closest of the dozen different taverns across the city where messages for her could safely be left.

"A memorable name," Laicos said. He hid the sneer, but Elathien could hear it just the same.

"Less a name and more a lifestyle," she said. "I also work alone." She smiled sweetly.

"And how do you know Master Cirhela?" Laicos was slipping into a mode of officiousness now, the anger quelled. Playing it safe for the moment.

"She's an old friend, who knows she can call on me when murder and dark magic are in the air," Elathien said. "Follow me and learn something."

The Blackheath badge in Elathien's possession got them past the mezzanine sentry at once, then past a pair of sentries at the top of the stairs. She knew that she was expected, but even the ease of her entrance made her return to Blackheath no less difficult. Whatever escort Laicos had been waiting for was quickly forgotten as they passed open office doors along the second-level mezzanine, clerks and adepts and healers nodding to them as they passed.

At the end of that second level, a set of double doors stood open, a sweeping spiral staircase rising up from the landing beyond. On the far side of the doors, Elathien slowed, looking up to where steps of white and black marble twisted through the bright light of evenlamps and the stark shadows between them.

"This is where it happened," she said.

"I read the report," Laicos replied dryly. "Written by the Guard patrol who were here last night, which I'm guessing you were not?"

Elathien ignored the investigator's question as she dropped to the floor, shifting her view to let the light pick out the details along the flagstones.

"In the patrol's report," she said, "did they talk about anything other than 'The Curse of Blackheath'?"

"What should the report have said?" Laicos's tone had a weary edge to it as he circled behind Elathien. "If you know this place well enough to have heard of the curse, you know why folk speak of it. Magic and madness congeal here, a hundred generations of it soaked up by the very stones."

"Except there is no curse. There never has been. Not like folk speak of it, at any rate." Elathien turned back to glance at the investigator before she stood, seeing his gaze suddenly shift. His movements suggested that he had been following her line of sight as she scanned the floor, but his eyes confirmed he had been studying her as she crouched in front of him.

"The curse of Blackheath is the excuse that lets others look away from things that happen in places like this. The patrol guards who were here last night made up their minds the moment they walked through the doors. Your captain did the same when he brushed off Cirhela's request for a full team of investigators."

"The Yewnyr Guard functions on process and protocol," Laicos said, "and one of those protocols involves grieving civilians not being the ones deciding where our resources are best spent. I'm here to make a full assessment of Master Cirhela's concerns…"

"Hang your protocol. I've done your job before, Laicos, and the truth is that the work that goes on here frightens people. Magic and madness. If it had been one of the inmates who died here last night, the Guard patrol likely wouldn't have shown up at all. The fact that it was a magister got them in the door, but misadventure is an easy call, so why bother looking for more?"

"And I assume that your purpose here will give you opportunity to answer that question at great length."

Elathien said nothing in response. She slipped a hand within one of the narrow seamed pockets on the inside of her broad leather belt, retrieving a folded piece of paper. This was the second item that had come to her before dawn that day, along with the silver badge. She held it out for Laicos.

"You're an investigator," she said, in a voice that she hoped left some room for doubt. "Tell me what you make of this." As Laicos took hold of the folded scrap as if it might be unclean, Elathien bent low again. She was looking for any telltale trace of blood on the marble. Whoever had cleaned up had done so a little too efficiently, though.

"Poetry," Laicos said. He had opened the paper and was assessing its dark lines of charcoal pencil dismissively. "A diary perhaps. Kept by a schoolgirl, to judge by the script and the content."

"Read it," Elathien said. She noted the fresh scratches along the stones where they'd been scoured with pumice. In a place such as Blackheath where spellcasters were common on the payroll, minor magic would normally have been entrusted to clear the blood from the marble. The signs of manual labor meant that magic hadn't been enough — which meant there had been a dweomer, some trace of magical power, in the blood itself.

"Everyone that once stood above will come to ground." Laicos was reading the page aloud, though that hadn't been Elathien's request. His tone was mocking. "Spared none of the pain that you refuse to feel. None of the hate that seeks your life out, hopes to kill it someday. Wash you with the tears you never cried, watch you fall from your high places, shattered against blind stone."

Elathien didn't need the recitation. She had memorized the words by lamplight that morning, before she set out for the Seven Winds' patio before dawn.

"It's a description of what happened last night when a magister fell from Blackheath's fifth floor," she said, looking up again to the distant top of the staircase as Laicos handed the note back.

"I read the report," he said. "I fail to see the need for a summary in blank verse."

"This wasn't a summary." Elathien folded the note and slipped it back to her belt. "It was written two days ago."

Laicos raised an eyebrow at that. "If you're suggesting divination, the lack of specific detail is troubling. And whatever the case, why wasn't this passed on to the Guard patrol who responded to the death if it might be related?"

A woman's voice came from behind them. "That was my fault, I'm afraid."

Laicos looked first, Elathien feeling an unexpected reservation as she turned. Wearing the black robes of a master of the refuge, the woman approaching them from across the sheltered landing was watching her.

"I'm Master Cirhela," she said. "Thank you both for coming."

"Master Cirhela," the young investigator said with a nod. "As a first order of business, would you mind confirming that this woman is here at your invitation? And what role exactly you expect her to take in this investigation?"

"Elathien," the master healer said, stepping in for a brief kiss on the cheek. Elathien hesitated as she half-returned it, Cirhela already turning away. "Yes, she is here at my invitation, and her role of course will be only to assist the Guard in its inquiries. I believe she has skills and unique experience that will be an asset to you. While you are here, you should please consider her a part of the refuge's staff for the purpose of maintaining full control over your investigation. We will, of course, cover your time and expenses."

The last was directed to Elathien, who heard the edge in her own voice despite her best effort to cover it. "You don't owe me anything."

Cirhela brushed a strand of dark hair back from her face. A habitual motion when she was worried, Elathien knew. The healer was half-a-head taller than her and fuller-framed by far. Nearly the height of Laicos where the young investigator spoke to break the uncomfortable silence that hung between the two women.

"Master, if I may. You said the information in this note was not reported?"

Though it had been nine months since she had last seen the master healer, Elathien's memory was quick to draw on the images of the time she and Cirhela had known each other. A year in Blackheath. Three months afterward. The easy way in which Cirhela hid her fear was a thing Elathien remembered from those days.

"It was reported," Cirhela said, as her almond eyes finally flicked away from Elathien's. "But I made the mistake of saying that the note was written by a convalescent here. The sergeant of the squad who responded to our call last night took an ill view of the visions of the mad. His words. I hope and trust that you'll be more open-minded."

From somewhere high above, a faint cry rang out. Something less than a scream, a man's voice twisted through with pain but empty of whatever emotion that pain might once have inspired. Only Laicos glanced up, the staircase empty above them.

"The initial investigation has made a preliminary supposition that Magister Sirnos's death was accidental," Laicos said. "If my investigation here gives me reason to suspect otherwise, I will, of course, recommend that the inquiry be expanded."

Elathien laughed, as much at the tone of controlling confidence in the young investigator's voice as at the words themselves. "Sirnos accidentally dismembered himself before hurling the pieces of his own body down a four-storey staircase to the floor?"

"What was left of the magister's body was suffused with dweomer," Laicos said sharply. "As you'd know if you'd read the preliminary report. Blackheath deals with some of the most powerful magic in the Elder Kingdoms. Dark mana, curses, spellcasters driven mad and channeling the raw essence of evocation and necromancy."

He was reciting from memory, Elathien guessed. That initial report, passing judgement for the sake of expediency as was the way of the Guard. "So you've already made your decision."

"I've weighed the evidence at hand," Laicos said coldly. "The most important fact of which is that accidents are a way of life at Blackheath. Four deaths in the past year, the most recent a month ago." He looked to Cirhela, who merely nodded. "Magister Sirnos made no reports detailing fear of assault or threats on his life," the investigator continued. "And were this a random attack, one would be hard-pressed to guess at what kind of assailant could so effectively murder a spellcaster of the magister's experience and power."

Elathien had stepped away, pacing around so that she was behind Laicos when she spoke. "The first order of any investigation is to separate all that feels false from all that feels true," she called out, "but to never forget that the line between truth and falsehood wavers like the shadow of sunlit clouds. What is set aside is never thrown away, and what is dismissed to the darkness should be regularly exposed to the light of second thought and reason."

Laicos turned toward her, his expression dark. "From the *Manual of Investigation and Evidentiary Deduction* by Bellas," he said. Elathien had quoted the legendary captain commander whose tactics of analysis and forensics had shaped the work of Yewnyr's Guard Investigators ten generations before. "The primary sourcebook for the investigator's art, and you're assuming I wouldn't recognize it?"

"Based on your analysis of the magister's death so far, I'm frankly astounded that you've even heard of it," Elathien said with a smile.

Cirhela stepped in between the two before Laicos could respond. "Investigator Laicos, I would like you to observe a convalescent here. The person who wrote the fragment that Elathien showed you. I think it might help your assessment of this investigation, as a means to determining whether the inquiry be expanded, at your recommendation."

Laicos kept his gaze fixed firmly to Elathien's as he weighed Cirhela's too-obvious attempts to placate him. Against her own best instincts, Elathien felt a familiar rush of pleasure in the young investigator's anger, so comically easy to provoke. She almost hoped for an equally angry response from him, but he found his professional demeanor in the end.

"Of course, Master Cirhela. Lead on please."

Elathien was careful to walk behind him, so that he couldn't see her shaking her head as Cirhela took them up the stairs.

— THREE —

IN THE SITTING ROOM with low chairs and floor cushions, white-painted tables and the painting of sunflowers, a girl stood in a convalescent's grey gown. Her rough-cut hair was the color of beaten copper, highlights of gold showing in the wan morning light at the tall windows beside her. The plaster of the ward's adjacent walls showed the marks of time and the touch of countless hands. But if anyone had looked closely, they would have seen a faint glimmer show through the grime.

Cirhela, Elathien, and Laicos watched the girl from the other side of that wall, the spell that opened the room beyond to their viewing showing as a milky window framed in translucent white. They stood in a narrow meeting room designed just for such observance. Its half-dozen chairs were all set to face the wall that had been blank when they came in, Cirhela using a charm of mithral she wore at her wrist to show what lay beyond it.

"Her name is Nerani," Cirhela said. In the way that the healer spoke, Elathien heard a familiar compassion. "She came to Blackheath a week past, showing signs of delirium and of the traumatic hold of powerful arcana. Her physical health was poor, but healing had no effect against whatever curse held her. She's gotten some strength back, but we have no idea yet what caused her trauma, let alone any sense of how to reverse it."

Unseen from the other side, the magical observatory cast the features of the girl in a pale light. Other convalescents shifted past her from time to time, but she stayed motionless at the windows, staring out and whispering unheard words. If she knew that the three of them were watching her, she gave no sign of it that Elathien could see.

"Where did she come from?" Laicos asked.

"We don't know."

Even with the shifting light through which they viewed her and the dark lines of her eyes that spoke to a lack of sleep, Nerani was blessed with a natural beauty that Elathien noted. A glance to Laicos where he watched intently suggested that he had noted it as well.

"I mean what information do we know? Who brought her here?" Though they had only begun to watch through the shimmering wall, Laicos was already showing impatience.

"No one brought her here," Cirhela said. "This is the mystery of Nerani. She was found inside the refuge at dawn, wandering the still-locked corridors."

"Blackheath is said to be one of the most secure sites in all the Free City," Elathien said. Like the others, her voice was hushed within the bare white walls of the meeting room, despite the fact that there was no chance of them being overheard by the slender figure they watched. "Is it really that simple a matter to break in?"

"To our dismay, yes. Our efforts have always been focused on preventing escape. Our sentry sergeants and masters of security have guessed that she came in through the kitchens. The Masters of Administration have since undertaken additional security at all entrances."

"And how many entrances are those?" Laicos asked.

"The main doors bring in visitors and new admissions. There are two side entrances, used by the healers and sentries, laborers and other workers."

"Making it equally likely that she was brought here in secret by one of those healers, sentries, or laborers." Laicos's tone betrayed a confidence more than a little out of step with the obviousness of the supposition, Elathien thought. "Someone's sister," he continued. "Someone's lover, possessed by dark spellcraft. Her family needed to cover it up for reasons that don't require an investigator to determine. Question your workers with truth magic and this so-called mystery is solved…"

"Except I can assure you that no one associated with Blackheath is friend or family to this girl," Cirhela said.

"Because whether you know where she came from, you already know who she is," Elathien said. Through the scrim of magical light, she was focused on Nerani's lips, trying to read the faint sense of the words there.

"Why would you say that?"

"My skills and unique experience," Elathien said simply.

The master healer's role here, the size and scope of the pain and horror that Blackheath dealt with on a regular basis, made it impossible to maintain even a minimal level of emotional involvement with the refuge's nearly two hundred inmates. But from among that number, Cirhela had always seemed unerring in her ability to pick out the ones she could care for. The ones not so far gone that her caring might help speed the healing process.

"Explain," Cirhela said.

"If she's been here only three days, you wouldn't have had time to care as much as you obviously do." Not inmates, Elathien corrected herself. *Convalescents,* she heard Cirhela's own voice say in her memory. *There are no inmates here.* It was the first thing the healer had said to her, a long time ago now.

"If my work here is interrupting whatever reunion lies at the heart of this conversation, I could perhaps return at another time." As he moved closer to the shimmering observatory, Laicos's tone was almost petulant.

"Forgive us," Cirhela said. "Elathien is correct. I know this girl. More to the point, I know her sister, who was a convalescent here before her. Irandis was her name. Nerani's twin."

"Was a convalescent," Laicos said. "Where is the sister now?"

"Dead." In Cirhela's voice, Elathien felt the sadness that told of more than just a professional loss. "Irandis took her own life here, nine days past."

Laicos's interest in the girl was broken with unexpected speed and force. The young investigator made the moonsign, scribing the twin crescents over his heart meant to ward against evil as he stumbled back from the window. "A girl dies in a place as rich in magic as Blackheath, and days later her double appears on the same spot? Have you stopped to consider what manner of creature this could be?"

Elathien laughed outright at that, Laicos's gaze on her as sharp as the sidesword that his hand had strayed to as a sign of his inexperience. It was a street guard's reaction, showing none of the caution that the investigator's trade demanded.

"A place as rich in magic as Blackheath? Laicos, there are likely more healers, more adepts and scholar-wizards under this single roof than at any other location in all the Elder Kingdoms. Do you honestly think that some undead shade or changeling could take up residence here without them knowing it?"

The anger in Laicos's expression showed that he recognized the severity of his gaffe, and that he was running out of patience with Elathien's manner. Before that anger could fuel a response, Cirhela spoke up.

"And even beyond our testing, there are proofs more mundane," she said. "Nerani is no double to Irandis, as alike as they were. Irandis was slighter than her sister, and shorter by a hand's width. She had a malnourished look to her, and most likely a childhood of poverty that stunted her. Nerani is healthier by far, though the health of her body has no bearing on the injuries of her mind."

"What's wrong with her?" Elathien said as she stepped to the image filtering through the wall, ignoring Laicos where he fumed behind her.

"We don't know. Divination and enchantment are used to open up the minds of convalescents who cannot know their own thoughts. But in Nerani's case, all her memories, all her thoughts are chaos. Her past is gone. All she knows and can think on are the events since she arrived here three days ago. That and one thought overriding all others. Love for her sister, Irandis."

"How did she die?" Elathien said. "Irandis?" She stared close at the glamered window, something tantalizing familiar in the unheard movement of the girl Nerani's lips. Whatever she was saying, she was repeating it. A refrain of a few sentences. A snatch of a song, perhaps. An incantation?

The hesitation in Cirhela's voice told Elathien as much as the response itself. "She fell to her death, from a window in the laboratories. The same way that Magister Sirnos…"

"Enough." Laicos waved a hand before Elathien, as though he thought that both she and the distant girl might suddenly disappear if he only willed it with enough force. "My apologies, Master Cirhela, but Magister Sirnos is my only concern. And this girl and her fragment of poetry appear to be scant evidence in the matter of his death."

"Investigator Laicos, until Nerani appeared, I had no idea that Irandis had a sister. Nerani was never mentioned in the time that Irandis spent here. There was no mention of her in the diviners' records. Irandis was brought here by the City Watch as a derelict, found wandering Anduras Hamlets in a state of catatonia that responded to no healing. A deep trauma, likely magical in nature, even as it eluded all our attempts to discern its cause."

"I am not investigating the death of an inmate," Laicos said coldly. "As such, I have no possible interest in her life."

"Irandis was here a month, but no one came seeking her. But when I talked to Nerani the morning she was found within these walls, it was as though she knew me. She knew details of Irandis's death that she should not have known. Where it happened, the time of night. The fact that Irandis had access to the Laboratory Tower that night because of a lock improperly set. And if she knew these things regarding her sister's death, I believe that her note might have been a vision of Magister Sirnos's death. A warning…"

"My time is wasted here." Laicos nodded to Cirhela and ignored Elathien in a single motion. He opened the meeting room door, light spilling in from the evenlamps of the corridor beyond. "If anything other than happenstance and supposition in the matter of the magister's death comes to light, contact the Guard and the investigators' office." Then he turned on his heel and was gone.

Elathien felt a moment of proper disdain sharpen the edge of her complete indifference toward the investigator. However, her mood softened when she registered Cirhela's quiet anger behind her.

"I was hoping that by your being here, you might have helped me get him to take this matter seriously," the healer said evenly. "I wasn't expecting you to actively drive him away."

"The most help he can give to an investigation here is by walking out the door. He's a second-rate bravo given a badge he hasn't even begun to earn, and the fact that the Guard Investigators gave the assignment to him means they had no intention of ever taking this matter seriously. They know Blackheath's reputation and they want nothing to do with it."

"And there's no chance at all that this is old hostilities clouding your judgement?"

"I have enough current hostilities to cloud my judgement," Elathien said with a smile. "I haven't needed to bother with the old hostilities in quite some time."

She stepped to the still-open door, turning opposite to the direction Laicos had headed loudly toward the stairs. In the meeting room, the shifting pane of arcane light continued to show the sitting room beyond. The girl was still at the windows, but she was pacing now. Shifting side to side as she ran her fingers along each lower sill.

For just a moment, as Nerani turned at the end of her repeated pathway, Elathien felt the girl catch her eye. Staring up at the wall as if she knew she was being watched from the far side of it.

Elathien blinked. The girl had continued onward, staring out through the windows again. Just her imagination, she thought.

"Come on," she said to Cirhela. "We've got work to do."

From the doors to the ward sitting room, snatches of faint voices that had gone unheard through the observatory at the wall rose and fell now, though their words remained indistinct. Elathien counted ten convalescents scattered across the room, four healers and adepts working with them. A quick glance might have given the impression of some academy classroom, or the common room of one of the monastic orders that dotted the Elder Kingdoms. A sense that the healers and those they worked with were peers, working together to ease the burden of trauma.

Elathien knew that the sentries never set foot into the ward rooms, an important part of the attempt to create a sense not of confinement but of safety. Convalescents, never inmates, notwithstanding that Elathien knew the vast majority of those who entered the refuge would never leave again. Dark magic. Ancient curses. Powerful undead and monstrous aberrations. The victims of all these things were the legacy of Blackheath, their minds and spirits shattered.

Nerani had her back to the windows now, staring at the white wall opposite. Though her mouth still moved, she spoke all but silently, the whispered words a thing she focused on with grave intent. Light from behind cast her face in shadow, a strange translucence to her complexion complementing the unblemished tones of the grey shift that she and all the other convalescents wore.

"I assume you want me to hang back while you talk to her?" Elathien asked, but Cirhela shook her head.

"On the contrary, I'd like to gauge her reaction to you. She's talked too much to me, I think. Her focus comes and goes, but even when she's focused, she's frightened. She pulls back. I think a fresh face might help her. As will your own sense of what she might have been through."

"I can question criminals well enough, but talking to convalescents isn't exactly what you'd call a proficiency."

"I'm sure you still remember a few things."

The healer's statement carried unspoken sentiments, but Elathien simply nodded. She followed cautiously as Cirhela approached the girl.

"Nerani. This is a friend of mine." Cirhela pressed close to the window, taking the girl's hands in hers. The wide-open eyes stayed fixed on the wall as the whispering faltered, then stopped. Elathien confirmed a repeated refrain as she approached, but she couldn't catch enough of the faint voice to place the words.

As she stepped through the girl's line of sight, Elathien felt the faintest touch of trepidation. She was hesitating, she realized, some kind of pressure diverting her from the girl's bright eyes. Something there she was afraid to see. She had to force her own eyes up to the emptiness in that green gaze.

"Nerani, my name is Elathien." When she smiled, it was with unexpected difficulty. "It's good to meet you."

The faintest movement in Nerani's eyes told Elathien that the girl was listening. With no sense of having anything to gain by hiding her purpose, she chose a direct approach.

"I was interested in the words you wrote down for Master Cirhela, three days ago. Do you remember? Can you tell me more about them?"

The girl's eyes focused on Elathien only for a moment before angling back to the wall. She shook her head. While Elathien, Cirhela, and Laicos watched from the meeting room, Nerani's arms had rested at her sides. Now they were folded across her belly, each hand clutching the opposite wrist.

"I sensed anger in the words," Elathien said. "Words that carry such anger can hurt us, whether we mean them to or not."

The girl's fingers shivered suddenly. Each flexed and slackened in turn, blunted nails digging into pale skin. Elathien resisted the urge to reach out and stop her.

"Blackheath hasn't changed much since I was a convalescent here…"

Elathien was surprised to hear herself say the words. It wasn't a confession she'd be planning to make, if only because she had no reason to believe that doing so would serve any purpose. But even as she spoke, she saw the girl's gaze flick back to hers, a point of recognition seen there.

"All this light," Elathien said. "All these walls of white, but there's a shadow here at all times. Not all of us feel it, but I did."

It was easy to assume that the blank stare was for the sake of trying to look beyond. But Nerani had been looking entirely inward, an experience Elathien remembered.

The girl began to whisper again. The same words as before, but Elathien recognized them this time.

Everyone that once stood above will come to ground…

"Do you feel it, too?"

Nerani's hands rose to the window suddenly, striking hard for the glass but instead slamming against the unseen shield of force magic protecting that glass. Her fingers flinched as the strength of that dweomer seized them, forcing a tremor down her arms that sent her stumbling back.

Cirhela moved to catch her but Elathien was faster, shifting so that the trembling girl fell into her arms. Across the chamber, eyes drifted toward them as Nerani cried out. Cirhela pressed close to her and Elathien both, whispering the words of an incantation that calmed the girl.

Most faint, Elathien caught the healer's scent, a memory of rose and lavender that should have been nothing but pleasant. It carried a threatening edge now, twisting in with the faint keening as the force field shivered and returned to its normal state.

Elathien shivered despite herself. She remembered the splintered pain of those windows only too well.

"She should return to her room," Cirhela said. "This is too much for her…"

Elathien cut the healer off. "Listen."

Held tight against her breast where it felt like she might otherwise fall to the ground, Nerani was whispering again. But Elathien heard a change in the words, pressing her ear close to the girl's mouth.

"The low heights…" Nerani whispered. "A house of fourteen lights. Please don't take me, please don't take me back…"

Elathien caught Cirhela's eye, the puzzled look there telling her that the healer didn't recognize the words. Nerani's voice rose, a suddenly frantic note twisting through it.

"The low heights, the fourteen lights… Fourteen lights…" Then the erratic mantra stopped as suddenly as it began.

The girl stiffened as she broke from Elathien's grasp, both of them standing as Nerani stepped back. Her eyes were clearer now, but blank where they met Elathien's gaze. No recognition.

"What does that mean, Nerani? What is the house of fourteen lights?"

"Don't take me…" The girl's voice was weak in response. Afraid.

"Perhaps we can…"

"Don't take me back!"

Her scream echoed from the white walls, cutting all other sound in the ward sitting room to silence. All eyes were on them, but Elathien was aware only of Cirhela's gaze, and the faint nod that directed her toward the door.

She stepped away as the healer escorted the shaking girl toward a concerned-looking adept watching from across the chamber. Together, the two of them walked Nerani through the expanse of staring faces, leading her toward her room. The narrow doors to the ward cells were open, but all Elathien could focus on were the squared-off slates beside each, marked in white chalk. She remembered her own name on a slate just like them. But try as she might, she suddenly couldn't remember which ward, which of Blackheath's top four floors had been hers.

She turned away quickly, slipping out of the sitting room and into the corridor beyond.

— FOUR —

WHERE SHE WAITED down the corridor, Elathien let herself fall back behind the flow of bodies that passed around her. Convalescents and healers, attendants carrying baskets of linens and gowns, kitchen staff with trays laden with bowls and pots of steaming soup and fresh-baked bread, and all of them under the always-watchful eyes of the sentries who patrolled the corridors at a steady clockwork pace. It was quiet, though. A kind of uncertain calm always hanging in the refuge despite the amount of activity that threaded through the halls.

A hustling worker passed her with a basket heaped high with dirty dishes, all of them carved in wood. No implements of metal were allowed anywhere on the wards. Another detail Elathien remembered.

"I'm sorry," she called out. She recognized Cirhela's footsteps approaching from behind even before she turned back.

The master healer slowed to let a group of convalescents under the escort of two other healers pass her. "It wasn't your fault," she said as she drew closer. "In fact, I was impressed by your approach. You got close to her as well as anyone on staff here would have."

"So I guess I do remember a few things," Elathien said, but she didn't return Cirhela's smile. "At least we have something to start with."

Cirhela gave her a quizzical look. "The low heights and a house of fourteen lights? What does that mean to you that it doesn't to me?"

"The Low Heights is Thaelind Heights, on the Ridge. Or at least that's what it's called by folk on the Ridge, to differentiate it from Abalendra Heights above it." Both names belonged to two of the upscale wards along the mountainous slopes of the northeast. The Free City pushed upward to its most exclusive summit there, marking the residences of nobles and merchant lords and the gentry of Yewnyr.

"It's been a while since I was invited to the Ridge," Cirhela said with a smile. "I apparently travel in the wrong circles."

"I'm betting it's been longer for me," Elathien said with complete honesty. "And you haven't missed much."

"But what are the fourteen lights, then?"

"No idea. But you should ask the ward healers and adepts, anyone who's worked with Nerani. Maybe it's something they recognize."

"It'll have to be later, but you're welcome to speak with them yourself. Magister Sirnos's death has the Council of Masters in emergency meetings that I'm already late for."

"Go then," Elathien said. "That'll give me a chance to access Magister Sirnos's chambers in the meantime."

"Of course. I'll speak to the sentry sergeant to arrange an escort for you."

"Or," Elathien said thoughtfully, "your keys could have gotten misplaced at some point this morning." She caught the uncertainty in the healer's look. "Just for a short while."

From somewhere farther down the ward, a voice sounded out suddenly. A dusky Ilvani was ascending the twisting staircase, her arms locked tight to the healer escorting her as she sang.

"I work best alone," Elathien said, conscious even as she did of how well Cirhela knew it.

"If you're caught, it means trouble for us both."

"I only get caught when I want to be."

The tone and cadence of the Ilvani's song placed her origins somewhere deep in the ancient forests, and the courts of the Ilvanrand that dwelled there. Her voice was beautiful beyond measure, the light of madness bright in her eyes as she passed along the corridor. Elathien was distracted from watching, however, as Cirhela leaned in close to embrace her.

The healer held her for a long moment that Elathien knew had two purposes. Against her own intent, she felt herself slipping into the familiar warmth of Cirhela's body, the scent of rose and lavender. She felt the healer's hand begin to tremble at her back before she reluctantly disengaged.

"Good luck," Cirhela said. Elathien merely nodded as she watched her turn for the stairs. The master healer's key was tucked into her palm, having been slipped carefully from Cirhela's hand as she broke away.

She made her way to the Master's Tower by a circuitous route, her memory of Blackheath's corridors and stairs a less than trustworthy blur. The wards of the fifth floor were virtually indistinguishable to Elathien's eye, and she began more quickly than she liked to feel the weight of the general atmosphere and the sameness of sentries and convalescents, the unadorned grey differentiated only by the sentries' dark green sashes.

In the end, she oriented herself around the single landmark of the upper levels that she remembered. Between the four circular towers that rose at each corner of the refuge like fingers reaching for the sky, an expanse of garden spread. Open to the air, it filled the space of the flat roof between the towers, and was marked by low stone walls along that roof's edge.

The garden was a place of retreat and relaxation for convalescents and the workers of Blackheath alike. In the time before, Elathien had first come here at Cirhela's invitation. However, as the process of her healing had progressed, she had earned the right to walk the broad green lawns and sit beneath their bright statues alone.

The lushness of the rooftop's flower beds and its sweeping stands of alder and sweet pine spoke to the power of druidic magic laid into the garden's foundations. In spring and summer, the trees leafed out along uncounted branches to weave a net of green against the sky, shading gravel paths and close-cropped green lawn, beds of columbines and heather, cranesbill and shrub roses. In winter, the trees were bare, their black bark touched with the same frost that streaked the tempered glass of the garden's broad doors.

From the garden, four entrances opened up to the four tower stairs of Blackheath, each set with wide glass doors and wider windows that showed the frosted gravel paths beyond. From the garden entrance to the Master's Tower, Elathien found the corridors she remembered. She easily ignored the looks she received from the healers and sentries she passed, Cirhela's silver badge set prominently on her shoulder to deflect any inquiries as to her business. Once on the upper levels, she found herself alone.

Cirhela's key carried a dweomer of magic set to match and open the magical locks of the institute's doors. Still, the areas of Blackheath to which the master healer's rank granted her access didn't include the suites of her fellow masters, so that the lock at Sirnos's door was resistant to the key's touch. Elathien expected this, however, and the lockpicks she pulled from one of her belt pockets took easy advantage of the way Cirhela's key could still help her read the magic of a lock it was unattuned to.

Darkness draped the empty office as Elathien quietly closed the door behind her. Carefully, she pulled back the grey drapes at the windows, letting in a haze of dusty daylight through which she appraised the books and scrolls spilling from the magister's voluminous shelves. With a whispered word, she cast a cantrip of detection, seeking magic along those shelves but not expecting to find any. Whatever scrolls and other arcana Sirnos kept here would have been cleared out already by the mages who answered to him, too valuable to be left among the magister's mundane works.

An unlocked door set between bookshelves opened up on a small bedchamber, Sirnos apparently one of the dedicated masters who lived full time within the institute. Elathien channeled her spell across a crisply made bed, over tables stacked with more volumes, three still laid open as if Sirnos might have just stepped out in the middle of some bit of research. She scanned framed diplomas and awards along the walls to match those she had already seen in the outer office, each testifying to the level of mastery with which the magister's work at Blackheath had been carried out.

Then she ignored all these things in favor of the great black desk that sat at the center of the outer office, and which was the only item in the magister's suite to radiate a steady pulse of magical dweomer.

Twice, Elathien paced around it, just looking. Then she took a moment to clear her mind, feeling her senses slip carefully out into the room around her. Letting her feel as though she was part of this place. Though she knew that any sorcerer of Sirnos's reputation should have been wary of leaving secrets exposed in so obvious a place as his office, she knew also that a sorcerer of Sirnos's power would hide any manifestations of that power as close to his person as possible.

She knelt to carefully inspect the desk, one surface and edge at a time. The old habits of her trade saw her bring out one of the long-knives she kept in matched hip scabbards hidden beneath jacket and cloak. Each as long as her forearm, the blades were Ilvani weapons equally as effective at range and in close combat. Elathien's present need was more mundane, however, as she pressed the razor-thin tip of a knife to the seams of each locked drawer, checking for and noting the traps she knew were there.

As she also expected, the magic she had sensed in the magister's desk was shaped specifically to keep someone like her out of it. The incantation of detection flared in her mind again, showing the strength and location of the desk's steady pulse of dweomer. In response, Elathien quickly marked out in her mind a best approach to the complex job of bypassing those magical defenses.

As a magister set atop a hierarchy of healers, Sirnos was powerful in spellcraft to a point where he would have both feared and trusted it above all else. Elathien had seen that mindset before, and as with others of his kind, Sirnos's trust and fear dictated the strength and scope of his defenses — layers of careful arcana that left him open to the less subtle approaches of a well-rounded thief.

As she did with so many of the things available to the folk of the Free City, Elathien had embraced the intrigue and wonder of magic from a young age. However, her parents' insistence that she take up her people's formal study of the spellcasting arts had all but guaranteed she would seek out only the most practical and illicit measures of magic's power. Never caring enough to seek the greater power in its most formal applications, her own spellcraft could sense the location and strength of Sirnos's magical wards, even as it had no power to break those wards. For that, she trusted to the keenness of her eyes and hands, and the subtle strength of the lockpicks that were her calling card.

Three times, she countered the strength of Sirnos's spellcraft with dexterity and steel. Three drawers she opened in turn, carefully inspecting the sheaves of parchment within for additional protections or magic before she brought them forth. Their contents were as routine as she had expected, running the range from mundane records of official expenditures and dealings with the government of the Free City, to notes on alchemy and spellcraft that she understood less than half of, to a half-finished and unaddressed love letter whose details made her queasy.

As she worked, Elathien tried to get a feel for the person who had once dwelled here. However, beyond the letter and the professional facade, Sirnos had left no sense of himself behind. The suite and its fittings held no personality, no warmth or emotion. It was a place that spoke of how its resident had seemingly lost some vital connection to life, even before the grisly end whose description had awoken Elathien before dawn.

And even as she scanned through the contents of the last drawer before restoring it, thinking about the magister's death forced Elathien to finally focus on the thoughts that had dogged her since even before her arrival at the refuge that morning. Thoughts that had been nagging at her since the knock had come at her door in the middle of the night.

It hadn't been a runner coming from Blackheath to her door. It had been Cirhela herself, cloaked and hooded where she stood on the threshold, pale and with fear in her eyes.

Cirhela was a master healer and warden of Blackheath. No stranger to death, nor to curses so dark that death might be a welcome release.

But whatever she had seen in the aftermath of Magister Sirnos's death had scared her like Elathien had never seen her scared before.

Leaning back on her haunches, crouched on the floor to observe the room from a different angle, Elathien felt a faint pinprick sensation rise along the back of her neck. It was a familiar feeling, and one that had served her well in her line of work. Something coming back to the senses she had let spill out into the room.

As she looked past the desk drawers, something shifted at the corner of her eye. When she looked back, it was gone.

With one eye closed, she held her hand up, blocking the right side of the desk to focus on the left. She measured it out against the length of a finger, then reversed the process, focusing on the desk's right side. Measured against the same finger, the bank of drawers to the right was higher, even as the number of drawers appeared the same to the naked eye that took both sides in at once.

She acknowledged the quality of the deception as she dropped to sit close to the desk's right side. An illusion reshaping form and space, its dweomer hidden within the stronger threads of protective magic. She closed her eyes, working by feel. The picks in her fingers traced out the lines of each drawer on the desk's right side, counting the three she had opened — and the one she had missed, hidden within a web of glamer between the desktop and the uppermost drawer.

She opened the secret space by touch alone, looking at the work only when it was done. The broken illusion was a haze to her eyes now. The hidden drawer seemingly pushed out from within the solid wood of the drawer below, blinking in and out of focus as her mind tried to adjust to this illusion of sight that couldn't be.

The interior of the secret space was lined with grey satin. Elathien peeled this back to confirm it as merely a covering for a further lining of lead foil, carefully bent and cornered. The thin sheath was proof against magical detection, an additional layer of obfuscation beneath the two layers of defensive and illusory dweomer already on the drawer.

Three items were held within. A sheet of worn paper, carefully folded. A black gemstone cracked along its rough facets, radiating a dweomer of evocation to Elathien's whispered incantation. And a thin sheath, also shaped of lead foil, a little larger in length and girth than both her thumbs set side by side.

She opened the sheath carefully where its edges had been folded over themselves, sealing whatever was held within. And as it opened, she felt the dweomer of the black gemstone fade and flicker — still there, but lost to her detection beneath a greater power.

Spilling from the lead sheath, magic surged within a sliver of blood-red crystal. Elathien felt her spell of detection react in warning as a dark power twisted through her. It set her fingers to shaking, so that she had to bring her hand to rest on the desktop for fear of dropping what she held.

Her lack of formal study of magic meant that Elathien's ability to glean insight into the crystal's function was limited. Still, she could read the raw dweomer well enough. Enchantment and necromancy, commingled in a way that made no sense to her. The magics of the mind, of darkness and death.

Where her shaking fingers traced the edges of the lead sheath, Elathien saw that it had been pressed down around the shard — and around two other shards just like it, to judge by the impressions left in the pliant metal. A set of three crystals had been stored within at some point, only one remaining now.

As Elathien sealed the sheath again, the dweomer faded. She felt a pain behind her temples that hinted at the intensity of the item's power, giving herself a moment to collect her thoughts as she turned her attention to the paper. It radiated no dweomer, even as its presence in the drawer suggested its importance.

She unfolded it carefully. She stared.

It was the same sheet that Cirhela had brought to her door that morning, along with her fear and a plea for Elathien's aid. The same words, written in the same angular script of dark charcoal pencil. *Everyone that once stood above will come to ground. Spared none of the pain that you refuse to feel…*

Except that the sheet of paper Cirhela had given Elathien was still in the pouch of her belt. She pulled it out carefully just to be certain, opened it to lay it side by side against the new. Studied together, the differences in form and layout between the two were noticeable even at a glance. The handwriting was tantalizing similar, though.

Then Elathien turned the new note over to see writing in another hand on the back. She had time only to register her surprise as the door to the magister's office swung wide.

"What is this outrage?"

The imperious tone of the Ilvani in the corridor was recognized a moment before Elathien remembered her face. The woman bore the placid visage and slender frame of the Elves of the Yewnwood, the same black master's robes that Cirhela wore hanging loosely on her.

"Lady Dacani." Elathien gave a half-bow, leading with the shoulder on which the silver Blackheath sigil badge was pinned. That movement covered her hand where she quickly folded both papers and slipped them to her belt. The master administrator's face was familiar to Elathien only through countless legal meetings that she had no interest in remembering now. It was not a face she had any interest in seeing again, on this day or any other.

"Elathien Solorilthae."

Her full name was something Elathien hadn't heard spoken in more than a year — the length of time since she was last in Blackheath. Dacani's recognition and memory impressed her, even as it grated more than she expected.

"Indeed. And so good to see you again," Elathien said, knowing full well that the dour Ilvani would take no more joy in this meeting than she would.

"You are trespassing in a secure tower of a private institution," Dacani hissed.

"I'm here at the invitation of Master Cirhela," Elathien said evenly, if not altogether honestly. "I've been asked to look into the untimely death of Magister Sirnos. I assure you, I'll be as unobtrusive as I can."

Elathien paced easily around the desk. She didn't know the administrator well enough to judge the full extent of her reaction, but she trusted that the venomous anger in Dacani's voice was entirely too real. It was an anger she found herself rising to, though she wasn't entirely sure why.

"The Yewnyr Guard are investigating the accident that cost the magister his life," Lady Dacani said darkly, "and that investigation remains no concern of yours, invitation or not. Master Cirhela has no interest in this matter, nor any right to bring in common criminals…"

"I am a former investigator of the Guard, Lady Dacani, and have extensive experience…"

"You left the Guard in disgrace, to which your arrest today will be a fitting coda. As director of this refuge, I will make it my mission to see you…"

"Correct me if I'm wrong, but the death of Magister Sirnos leaves Master Cirhela as the ranking member of the Council of Masters of the institute. Which is to say, holding rank over you. Seeking answers to murder by spellcraft would seem to be entirely within her purview."

"The sentries will be called. For the sake of avoiding scandal, I would suggest you be gone from these chambers and this refuge before they arrive."

Elathien noted a faint shift in the administrator's tone, underlining the sudden and significant backpedaling in her words. From the threat of arrest to being told to slink off to avoid scandal, coming in reaction to Elathien's understanding of the power structure at the refuge. An odd thing, she thought, even as she stared the administrator down for a moment.

"As you wish," she said with a shrug. She registered Lady Dacani's surprise, the administrator moving back in the doorway to allow her to step past. But as she did, Elathien turned, pressing close. "But when the sentries arrive, you should recommend that they seal the magister's chambers in advance of the Guard returning to take them apart, wall by wall, stone by stone."

As Elathien raised her left hand, the shard of crystal there flared blood-red in the light of the corridor's evenlamps. She had palmed the lead sheath after opening it one-handed. "I would expect a full squad of investigators at first, followed by the enforcers of the Authority Arcane. I can't imagine their inquiry will be anything less than destructively thorough."

She watched Dacani's eyes closely, but she caught no sense of recognition as the administrator glanced to the red-black crystal.

"What manner of pathetic bluff is this?"

"No bluff. This came from the magister's desk. Two more like it were once stored there, as any competent dweomer reading by the Guard or the Authority Arcane will prove." This was an almost desperate lie, Elathien's limited knowledge of magic giving her no way to even judge how close to the mark the bluff might be. However, she trusted that the bureaucrat Dacani's knowledge of spellcraft was even thinner in the end.

"You dare try to blackmail…"

"Blackmail? I'm an agent of the law, my lady. And this is dweomercraft banned by the laws of the Free City and of Gracia, which the absence of the necessary deeds of arcane bond makes most problematic for you."

This second lie was only slightly less egregious than the first, but to judge by the pallor that streaked Lady Dacani's expression, it had the intended effect. The arcane-marked deeds required to legally accompany all items of magic bonded for use in the Free City would have indicated that Magister Sirnos had authorized and registered both the gemstone and the crystal. And though such deeds could have realistically been stored anywhere for safekeeping, the fact that Sirnos had gone to such lengths to hide the objects suggested a need for secrecy.

Elathien circled close to where Lady Dacani stood in the doorway, not giving her a chance to respond to the threat in her tone. "This is necromancy and divination on a level I've never felt before," she said, "twisted in ways that suggests ten different types of forbidden lore. Depending on how forbidden, the Council of Masters will be first on the Authority Arcane's list of those dragged to the Tower of Law to determine whether they're guilty of knowing about Sirnos's illegal work. Or guilty of failing to discover and report that work."

Elathien turned away from the administrator's drawn face, walking easily down the corridor a half-dozen steps. Then she stopped. "Or, as an alternative, I could continue my investigation. Discreetly."

With her back turned, Elathien slipped the sliver of crystal back to its lead sheath and into one of the seamed pouches of her belt. She took no other precautions with it, knowing that despite its apparent fragility, the dweomer that threaded the relic made it stronger than steel. The note, folded one-handed, went after it. The cracked black gem had been safely palmed unseen in her other hand while Lady Dacani watched her. She slipped it now into the pocket of her cloak.

When she turned back, Dacani was closing and locking the magister's door. The administrator met Elathien's gaze with a look of dead contempt. But she said nothing else as she turned and stalked away.

— FIVE —

FOR MOST OF THE thousand-thousand citizens of the Free City of Yewnyr, the sunset was a thing suggested more than seen. Across the lower wards that flanked the river, the sky was all but blocked behind the city's walls and tightly twisting streets. Especially in winter, dusk and dawn were seen only as a shifting in the light, marked out by a surge of red across the sky.

Pacing through the ward rooms of the fifth level of Blackheath, Elathien could see that surge beyond a dark skein of cloud that had cut the winter day even shorter. After leaving Dacani, she had walked the rest of that day away, seeking out and questioning the sentries unlucky enough to have found Sirnos the previous night, along with the healers on duty on the upper floors.

The sentry who had found the magister's body was an Ilvani named Tajamynar, but the story Elathien pieced together from him and the others was a consistent tale of no one hearing or seeing anything suspect at that dark time. Sirnos had been observed at large in the refuge throughout the previous day, then had met with members of the council in his chambers before dusk. After that, nothing. In particular, the sentry Tajamynar would have seen Sirnos if he had been on the fifth level, having passed through those corridors only a short while before the magister's gruesome end.

Elathien was bound now for Cirhela's offices with the written records of her interviews, having seen neither her nor Lady Dacani nor any other black-robed master in the refuge over the balance of the day. Elathien didn't know what a council meeting in the aftermath of a magister's death would look like, but she expected it would likely run late. Passing through one of the many common rooms that connected the wards, she saw the corridor doors already closed, the refuge beginning the process of shutting down for the night. But as she glanced to the tall windows and the shadow of the sky spilling to the stone floors, Elathien slowed.

Standing motionless before the glass and its additional pane of shimmering force, the girl Nerani stood in silhouette, staring out at the city. An open space of battered chairs and low tables stood between them. Her back was to Elathien, her copper hair taking on the hue of the fading sunset sky.

From behind her, Elathien heard footsteps. An elderly convalescent appeared, a Human male shuffling past her in a white gown, his feet bare. The color of the gown indicated some measure of importance over and above the grey worn by most convalescents, Elathien knew. Along his arms, he wore the glowing tattoos of the Authority Arcane, Yewnyr's force for the detection, investigation, and destruction of dangerous magic. Blackheath was a place where all too many of the Authority Arcane's mages wound up in the end. This one's mouth moved, his expression thoughtful, but his voice and thoughts were long gone.

Elathien stepped to the side as he passed by and drifted through an open doorway, not seeing her. When she flicked her gaze from his retreating form back to the window, Nerani was watching her, no emotion in the girl's empty eyes.

Elathien knew that she should just walk away. She had no idea what state the girl might be in, nor did she have any urge to talk to her again without Cirhela there to oversee it.

"Hello, Elathien." Nerani's voice carried clear through the silence.

Elathien stood for a long moment. Then obeying an urge, an instinct, that she couldn't name, she approached at a slow walk.

At Nerani's back, the shimmering window reacted as she brushed against it, setting up a ripple of faint shadow. The girl's hands were clasped in front of her. "It's good to see you again," she said.

Elathien pulled a chair close, sitting to face her. She measured the awareness in the girl's voice, remembering and having difficulty comparing it to the uncertainty she had witnessed that morning.

"It's good to see you, Nerani." Elathien tried and failed to think of something else to say, adding only, "I'm sorry we couldn't speak longer this morning…"

"Did you know her? Irandis?" A measure of hope twisted through the girl's voice as she cut Elathien off, a hint of memory flashing in her blue eyes.

"I'm sorry, no. I didn't know her. Master Cirhela told me about her…"

"Are you a healer?" Past Nerani, the last light of dusk was fading at the window. Evenlamps along the marred white walls filled in the lengthening shadows with their pale glow.

"No," Elathien said. "No, I'm not."

"You speak like a healer."

She shrugged. "I've spent a lot of time talking to healers. The healers of Blackheath helped me once, as they try to help you. As they tried to help your sister." And even as she said it, Elathien realized that she was using Cirhela's voice. The soothing tone that had helped carry her out of the darkness two years ago.

"Did you know Irandis?" Nerani asked again as she half-turned to the window. She seemed confused suddenly, reaching up to brush the unseen protective field with a tentative hand.

"No. No, I didn't."

"But you know how she died?" The girl's fingers trembled at the touch of arcane that wrapped the glass. Her hand darted back, then pressed in again. A shiver twisted through her.

"Yes." Elathien hadn't meant to say it. She felt an unfamiliar uncertainty twist through the word, a reflection of the pain she heard in the girl's voice.

"Do you know where she died?"

"Yes."

Nerani reached down to grab the hem of her gown, wrapping it around her hand. She exposed both legs to the top of the thigh as she raised it, Elathien appraising her smooth skin with a critical eye. The girl showed no signs of the unwashable grime, the faintly layered scars that came with living rough on the streets, even though every other part of her appearance spoke to a life lost somewhere.

With her hand wrapped in thin cloth, Nerani pressed in against the screen of force, causing it to shimmer and twist away from her. The cloth would insulate the flesh for a short while from the unseen field, and from the arcane feedback that trained the convalescents of Blackheath to stay away from it. Elathien had tried that approach herself, more than once.

"Take me to where she died." With an angry thrust, Nerani pushed her cloaked hand through the field, driving it to strike the tempered glass of the window itself. A dull sound like a muffled crystal chime rang out as she staggered back, falling to her knees.

Elathien made to rise from her chair, instinctively wanting to help, but Nerani drew back even at the hint of her drawing closer. She was already feeling a sympathetic pain shooting through her own arm, saying nothing as the girl slowly stood.

"Take me to where she died." As she stood again, Nerani's voice was edged with a kind of defiance.

"I don't know if that would be wise, Nerani."

"I'll tell you what you want to know."

Elathien watched thoughtfully as Nerani turned back to the window, assessing carefully all the different ways she might respond. She wanted to ask what exactly the girl thought she wanted to know, even as she knew that doing so would divert the conversation from where Nerani was directing it.

"Even I wanted to take you," she said at last, "I'm not allowed to go there. All the towers are locked."

"But you have Master Cirhela's key."

From somewhere behind her, deep within the chambers where the mind-lost mage had drifted away, Elathien heard a cry of pain. Then a distant snatch of song came back as if in answer, a woman's voice, familiar somehow. The Ilvani she had heard earlier? She didn't know.

"Isn't that right?" Nerani asked, but Elathien said nothing in return. She only rose from the chair, walking toward the closed doors to the main corridor and the stairs beyond.

As she set Cirhela's key to the lock of those doors, Elathien looked back to see Nerani following.

The dweomered key made a faintly musical sound when it was fitted to the equally well-magicked lock of the entrance to the Laboratory Tower. A plaintive tone, like a child's voice faintly breaking the silence of sleep, the sound accompanied them through four more doors as Elathien and Nerani made their careful way up, passing no sentries on the way. Even with Cirhela's key and the master healer's silver badge on display, Elathien was glad to not have to bluff her way past anyone with the girl in tow.

As the final door opened, the darkness beyond was cut with light from the corridor, spilling into a space of tables strewn with glassware flasks and vials. The glint of metal reflected from equipment, only some of which Elathien recognized, sheaves of parchment scattered between them. Tall shelves of books and scroll tubes, reagents and powders held in dim glass jars were spread along the walls across from three high windows. The bright night of Yewnyr streaked the clouds as a distant gleam beyond the glass.

Darkened oil lamps were mounted at each corner of the room, but no evenlamps could be seen. Elathien guessed that the alchemists and healers who worked in this place would be wary of the effects of latent magic on the elixirs and tinctures they crafted. Having less reason to worry, she whispered an incantation that set one of those lamp brackets flaring with a golden light.

Behind her, Nerani entered slowly, then closed the door behind her. She leaned back against it as the lock clicked shut, a momentary weakness seeming to pass through her. Elathien watched, wary, but Nerani ignored her as she stared to the darkened windows.

"It was here," she said quietly.

"According to what Master Cirhela told me. Yes."

The girl stepped away from the door to circle the room slowly. She seemed to drink it in, her eyes and fingers touching every surface. She brushed the shelves, the tables, their carefully arranged configurations of scales and alembics and mortars as she passed.

"Nerani, do you know why you've come here? To Blackheath?" Elathien was keeping careful pace with her, watching the girl as she stepped close to the center window. The light of the room set her face into rippled reflection in the shadowed glass, the city unseen now beyond it.

Nerani set her hand to the glass, watching with a childlike intensity as her fingers touched down on its chill surface. "No magic here."

"No," Elathien said. "Not off the wards. Convalescents aren't allowed here." She said it carefully, watching for a reaction.

"Irandis was here."

"Someone made a mistake, Master Cirhela said. There was an emergency that night. The healers and the sentries were attending to it. Doors were left unlocked that shouldn't have been."

Nerani stepped back from the window but kept her hand there. Her fingers stretched out, eyes shut and face downcast.

"Is this what you want to know?" Elathien asked. "How it happened?"

As Nerani looked up, her red-gold hair framed her face, touched by shadow as she twisted to keep the lamp behind her. "I know how it happened. I felt Irandis die."

Elathien saw the trembling at the girl's fingers, working its way up her arm as if she might be feeding on the chill beyond the dark glass. "We should go," she said.

But Nerani broke away from the window with a start, turning as she paced into the light, then away from it, passing from brightness to shadow and back again with a dancer's grace.

"I felt the spell that traced through her that night to keep her from screaming," the girl said. Her voice was raw. "To keep her from knowing. They waited until the healers were gone, the sentries were gone. No one to help her. I felt how many times they threw her against the glass of the window. I felt how it cut her when it finally broke."

Elathien was forced to take a step back as Nerani turned on her suddenly. A dark strength had worked its way through the girl, giving her the tone and disposition of a different person. The thought set Elathien on edge as she called up the cantrip of detection, the incantation barely a whisper.

"She knew all their names," Nerani hissed, pushing closer. "She knew what they did, what they needed, how they lied. She wouldn't have told, but their fear blinded them. Made them not believe her. So I felt how long it took her to fall. How her legs broke, her spine shattered when she struck the ground. I felt her bleed to death in the dark…"

There was no magic in her. No sign of the possession or enchantment that Elathien would have sworn she was seeing, no sign of Nerani's thoughts or actions controlled by some outside force. With a sharp cry of pain, the girl pushed past her, stumbling toward the laboratory door.

Which was open now, Elathien saw.

The white light from the corridor beyond pushed up against the pale glow of Elathien's spell-light, shimmering along a boundary like oil and water settling slowly against each other.

The door had been closed when Nerani stepped away from it. A thousand things could have explained it opening, from the most minor incantation to a loose latch and a breath of air from the corridor beyond. Elathien felt a chill twist through her all the same, rising from the base of her spine as Nerani turned to her.

"They killed Irandis," the girl said. "You wanted to know."

"What?" Elathien's voice caught as she spoke. "I wanted to know what?"

"You wanted to know why I came here. To Blackheath."

Nerani's steps were steady as she made her way down the corridor, bare feet silent on the stone floor. Elathien watched until the girl disappeared into the haze of light and shadow ahead, then followed out of sight behind.

She retraced the route they had taken from the ward floor perfectly. In a corridor just beyond the exit from the Laboratory Tower, Elathien heard a raised voice ahead — someone seeing the girl at large and responding with incredulity and care in equal measure. Even at a distance, she recognized one of the healers on Nerani's ward from earlier that day. She was thankful for that as she followed them, watching unseen as the girl was gently returned to her rooms. The healer spoke to her in a hushed voice as they walked, and Elathien recognized the calming tone even if she couldn't make out the words.

She retraced her steps, then, returning to the laboratory. If someone had asked her in that moment, she wouldn't have been able to explain why.

Closing the door behind her, she dismissed her spell-light with a wave, sending the room into darkness again. Against that dark, the glow of the city shimmered at the windows, the edge of the skyline reminding her of the eight-storey distance down to the black streets below.

She stood there for a long while before she finally gave in to the urge to look out those windows. Staring down into darkness to the place where Irandis had fallen.

Elathien listened at the door for a time to make sure the corridor was clear before she stepped out. Then she checked that door with a careful sweep of touch, sight, and spell. There was no sign of any problems with latch or lock, no sign of anyone having followed the two of them. The dust in the corridor gave up its record easily enough. Two sets of prints, her boot tracks tracing alongside Nerani's bare feet. No one else had come behind them.

When she was done, she closed the laboratory behind her. She set the lock twice to ensure it stayed closed before she slipped away.

— SIX —

BLINDS CUT OF white linen were half-turned at the dark window, the white light of an evenlamp suspended from a brass fixture on the pale desk. It cast a bright pool across the carpeted floor and the bookshelves of Cirhela's offices, where the healer sat on a low couch close to the door. Elathien was leaning back against the desk, its light casting her face in half-shadow as she finished telling her story.

Cirhela could only stare in stark disbelief. "Irandis was murdered?"

Elathien shrugged. "So Nerani says, and with a fixation on details. Except that she has no way to know those details, and she's clearly suffering from some sort of trauma that likely would have seen her end up in Blackheath regardless of her connection to Irandis. She believes her sister was murdered. That's all I can say for certain."

Where the light trailed away to shadows as it touched Cirhela, Elathien thought she saw lines of worry on the healer's face that she couldn't remember from a year before. She had come to the office to explain the fact of Nerani being at large half the refuge away from her ward, knowing that the healer would hear it and not wanting her to worry. However, Cirhela's larger concern had been entirely for what Nerani had revealed.

"But you believe her." Though the healer's voice half-framed it as such, it wasn't a question.

"Why would you think so?"

As Elathien tried to recall Cirhela's face from nine months past, the last time she'd seen her, she was caught off guard by the realization that she couldn't. Where she dug deep, she felt only the shadow of memory. An empty space, into which the face of the woman sitting before her now didn't fit anymore.

"Because," Cirhela said, "if you thought it was delusion, it would have only reinforced what you'd already seen of her mental state. It wouldn't have added anything to what we know of Nerani, so you would have had no reason to tell me."

The healer's office featured the same high windows of the rest of Blackheath, but set between those panes were dozens of paintings in glassed frames. Pastorals and still lifes in watercolor, most of them done by Cirhela's own hand, lent a brightness to the room that cut the shadows.

"I believe that Nerani believes it," Elathien said. She felt the warmth of those framed images edge away a faint chill. "I believe that the anger in what she wrote was likely driven by that belief. But the questions of how she came by that belief and whether it connects to Sirnos's death remain fairly wide open."

As Elathien leaned back to slip a hand to her belt, Cirhela nodded, thoughtful. "Do you really think it was a good idea to take her up there?"

"No," Elathien said. "But it wasn't my idea."

When her hand came up, it held the red-black crystal and the cracked gem between her fingers. Cirhela rose to step closer, Elathien twisting the fingers of her other hand as she whispered the incantation of detection, opening up the magic of both relics to her mind. She shifted to put the evenlamp behind her, darkening the room to make that magic flare as a shimmering aura around both stones.

Cirhela spoke words of her own, the subtler weaving of movement and animys that let her read the auras with her own spellcraft. The healer's magic was different than Elathien's sorcery in every conceivable way, but the unknowable baseline on which all magic was shaped allowed the reading of dweomer with equal ease. The look of sudden shock on the healer's face told Elathien she felt the power in the blood-red crystal just as she had.

"What in fate's name is that?"

"No idea. But Magister Sirnos had it very well-hidden in his desk."

"Contraband?"

"Most likely. A dark secret at the very least, given that neither you nor Lady Dacani recognize it."

"Lady Dacani?" Cirhela's expression registered a different kind of shock, but no less emphatically.

"She showed up as I was looking around."

Cirhela was darkly thoughtful. "She has no business that should have taken her anywhere near Magister Sirnos's rooms. How did she know you were there?"

"An alarm would be my guess. Some bit of the magister's spellcraft that I missed."

"But attuned to Dacani's hearing? Why?"

"I don't know," Elathien said thoughtfully. "Just as I don't know why she would threaten me with sentries but not simply call them directly. Needing to see who was there before she could decide whether it was friend or foe." She shrugged. "The most obvious explanation is that Sirnos and Dacani were involved in some kind of clandestine relationship. Lovers, perhaps. She's spent time in his office, but likely has no more sense than you or I of what he might have been involved in or what happened last night."

"Those two, lovers? What a horrid thought."

"I'm sure this place has seen stranger pairings."

There had been no specific meaning in the comment when Elathien said it, but she saw how Cirhela had taken it in the sudden flash of her eyes. She was still holding the crystal, the healer reaching out to touch it, her fingers coming to rest against Elathien's hand.

"It'll take some time to make a proper reading of it," Elathien said. "Work out what it is, what it does."

"What of the other stone?" Cirhela refrained from touching the red-black crystal, but she took the cracked black gemstone in hand as she continued to weigh its magic in her mind.

"A stone of sending," Elathien said. "I've read this dweomer before. Sirnos must have been in the habit of speaking with someone whose conversations weren't meant to be overheard. It's useless to you or I now, but if we find the stone's mate at some point, its dweomer will prove the connection to this one."

As Cirhela moved closer, Elathien caught the healer's scent again, even more jarringly familiar in the silence that surrounded them. "I should have asked you this morning," Cirhela said. "Have you been well?"

"I have. And you?"

Cirhela kissed her in response. Elathien felt the touch of her tongue with a sudden rush of memory. She was light-headed suddenly, losing control in a way she didn't like. Under cover of stowing the black gemstone and the blood-red crystal in her belt again, she shifted her head. Cirhela lingered for only a moment before she turned away.

"What is next for you?" the healer asked "Your plan? I assume you have one?"

"Of sorts. I have some inquiries to make in the city, but I'll return in the morning."

Elathien was halfway to the door when she slowed. "What do you think happened to Nerani?" she asked. "For her to appear so suddenly, no thoughts of her own past. Love for her sister overriding all else." She glanced back to see Cirhela sitting at the desk, feeling something twist inside her at the look in the healer's eyes. The caring there summoned up a faint pain for her now.

"I don't know," Cirhela said.

"But you've thought about it. You have better insight into the physic and healing of the mind than any person I know. You must have a theory."

Cirhela nodded. "I do, but it's not one I like. For twins to both manifest such strong disorders of the mind, it points to a malady of blood and body. If that is the case, then Nerani might well have been subject to it first, even worse than Irandis when she was a convalescent here."

"Her health," Elathien said thoughtfully. "Her physical well being. She hasn't lived on the street, but you said she wasn't here."

"She was never at Blackheath, no. This I'm sure of. But there are other places. Worse places. Worse fates for ones such as her. Lost and adrift her whole life, and with no one to ever come looking for her."

Elathien felt for the shape of words in her thoughts, but a momentary darkness was all she could feel. A tremor threaded her hand where it touched the door, ready to open it, but she couldn't leave. Thinking only of the scent of rose and lilac pooling in the light around Cirhela where the healer watched her closely.

"I heard your name," Cirhela said to break the silence. "This summer just past, in connection with a sorcerer in Caldstream Ward keeping street children as slaves for his experiments."

The case Cirhela named had been one of the most daunting that Elathien had undertaken since rebuilding her once-shattered life. It had put her head to head against the Yewnyr Guard whose rank and order had once defined her life.

"How did you hear about it?" she asked.

"The survivors were brought here. The youngest had barely ten summers on him. We couldn't save him."

Elathien stood in silence for a long moment. "I'll be back in the morning," she said at last. "Send a runner if you need me before then." Then she slipped out the black door of the office and was gone.

Elathien paced the lamplit streets of Mirayth Ward for as long as the cold let her, drinking a flask of wine bought from a cart vendor working the shadows of the street's shuttered shops. As she walked, she saw the high walls of the working-class tenements shift slowly to more comfortable apartments the closer she got to the merchants' quarter in Rendel Hall.

She had explored these same streets with Cirhela more than once, in the course of the long healing in the aftermath of days that she refused to think about now. Even without thinking, though, the memory of those days still lingered at the edge of her mind, like a shadow persisting even after the figure that cast it had gone. Memories of the healing process. Memories of the family she hadn't seen since then, and of the small satisfaction that gave her.

The streets she was walking would take her eventually to the river, and one of the penny-ferries that ran to the north bank from the docks at Frey's Crossing. She was killing time because she knew that the gem merchant whose custom she sought wouldn't be stirring until the night had truly settled. His name was Argil, and his pawnbroker's shop in Jesana Wharf hid his business as a purveyor of illegal magic behind a front as a purveyor of only slightly less illegal antiquities.

It had been some time since Elathien had needed to make use of a divination of identification, one of the first spells she had ever learned. Magic locked into the material world was reluctant to yield up its secrets, and so those secrets came at a price — specifically, the price of a pearl whose destruction and consumption would shape her spell as it unlocked the red-black crystal's secrets.

 In exchange for spellcasting done in secret and beneath the scrutiny of the Authority Arcane, Argil sold Elathien pearls of high quality at his own cost. His windowless shopfront was marked by the sign of a sprite perched within a crescent Darkmoon, but those who traded there only ever called the place *Argil's* after its nocturnal proprietor. When Elathien arrived, he was already behind the counter, locking the door behind her to conduct business and engage in the overly complex bargaining that seemed to give him great satisfaction.

When it was done, she had used up a good portion of her day's remaining spell-strength in assessing the power and dweomer of three magic blades that had come into the pawnbroker's possession. They were Dwarven work of the Steelpeaks judging by their look, and by the phrase of command that Elathien's power gleaned from one of them. Two she had simply detected and read. In the third, she sensed power that needed a deeper understanding.

That was a war-priest's blade, possessed of a dweomer of healing whose worth went far beyond its combat strength, and which meant that Argil was definitely getting the better end of the bargain they struck tonight. Still, when she set out again a short while later, it was with six pearls tucked into her belt pouch, each of whose value would have paid the rent on her residence for the better part of half a year.

Though she wasn't hungry, Elathien reminded herself that she hadn't eaten since the morning. She took a last walk to the markets along Magdea Street, which spread in the shelter of the great yewn trees growing in arches up and over the cobbles. With a flatbread wrap of hot spiced lamb and winter greens in hand, she hailed a rickshaw for the long journey of broad streets and bridges across the city and back home. As she ate and finished the last of the wine, she admired the thickly muscled legs and back of the rickshaw's Essaruk runner, who wore only a fur loincloth despite the winter chill.

Elathien's flat was in Kardonhill Ward in the city's northwest, where folk tended to be wealthy enough to afford their security, but not wealthy enough that they got any enjoyment out of flashing that wealth around. Her building was set along a broad lane off Restion Street, but accessed only by private entrance along an alley adjacent to a tavern called the Broken Archer. Her narrow flight of stairs was set with arcane alarms of her own devising, but in the year that she'd lived there, she had yet to need them. She gave the locks at the door a cursory check for signs of unwanted activity, though. An old habit she had no intention of losing.

In the spare fragility of furnishings too rustic by far for the neighborhood, Elathien lit the fire and finished her meal. Her rooms were open and accessible, as she liked them. No sense of separateness or privacy dividing space from space, bedchamber from sitting room, sitting room from kitchen. With water heated at the fire, she stripped and washed, even as she heard the telltale sound of footfalls that told her Diranta was back from his nighttime rounds.

The dog's entrance and exit from the flat weren't the main door, but rather the open edge of the narrow terrace that adjoined Elathien's bedchamber by way of a low, top-hinged door she had had constructed in the larger entry to the terrace. From there, Diranta could leap gracefully to the garden portico of the apartments across the arms'-stretch width of alleyway below. That was the residence of a widowed Ilvani noble named Ghilana, who had a soft spot for the dog and likely fed him at least as often as Elathien did.

Elathien's terrace was magically alarmed as well against the presence of any creatures but Diranta and her. Moreover, the route the dog took through Ghilana's gardens descended three flights of stairs before opening up to the street, and was patrolled by the Ilvani matron's six bodyguards, all deadly knife-fighters of the Yewnwood. As such, Elathien had never experienced any worry about someone trying to follow the dog home.

Landing lightly on the terrace, Diranta made a beeline for the scent of lamb. Elathien had saved him a morsel that he waited patiently for as she dried herself.

"You look tired," she said, and it was true. He was flat on all fours before the fire, only his eyes showing any signs of life as they flicked from her to the food. "Nice to know one of us is getting some action." The dog gave her a quizzical look, then shot to attention as bread and meat were tossed toward him, both pieces snapped at once from midair.

Diranta was one of the water dogs of the Duchy of Staris, trained to run ropes to the fishing boats along that southern coast. However, the breed had long been more common in the north of Gracia as a pet for nobles and propertied families alike, their long coats too often curled and corded and combed out in ways Elathien found exceedingly grotesque. She allowed Diranta's jet-black hair to grow wild for the winter, layered now as thick ringlets that trapped the heat of the fire beneath her fingers. As she sat with him, she was conscious of the intelligence in his eyes, and as grateful as always for the silence that was their conversations.

She thought back through the events of the day, setting what she knew and didn't know into place in her mind. The investigator's rituals defined by Bellas had been committed to memory when she was a new recruit to the Yewnyr Guard, in her zeal to impress her trainers and sergeants. To impress her uncle, who had worn the badge of Captain that Elathien set her mark on once. Her uncle who had betrayed Elathien and that badge alike.

The shadow of memory again. Elathien stared to the light of the fire to push the dark away. And as she did, she let the girl Nerani's voice slip through her mind, remembering not just the words but the emotion that underlay them.

The low heights, the fourteen lights… From the look on the girl's face when she said the words, Elathien was quite certain that she had no idea why she'd said them. The moment hadn't held the feeling of magical compulsion, however — a thing Elathien often wished she had less familiarity with. An unwilling memory, then. Something from the past that was lost to Nerani, and to even the magic with which Cirhela and the healers of Blackheath had tried and failed to read that past.

A house of fourteen lights. Please don't take me, please don't take me back…

The Low Heights was Thaelind Heights on the Ridge. The rest, she'd have to discover.

First things first, however.

Elathien brought forth one of Argil's pearls, crushing it carefully in a pestle to a shimmering powder. As she had in the pawnshop when she plied the same magic for Argil's benefit, she poured a goblet of red wine, a bold red of the distant Cotanas Valley that held infinitely more pleasure than Argil's nameless city-vinted swill. She stirred it with the feather of an owl that she kept on a tall bookshelf only for that purpose, whispering the words of the divination as she did. She saw a pale light flare within the draught, setting her jaw against its bitterness as she drank it down for the second time that night.

The tincture fed the power of the spell within her, which set a shadow across her sight with a single point of clarity at its center. The red-black crystal shone at that center, set out against white cloth on the sitting room table. Elathien felt the crystal's power thread through her, the same strange weave of dweomer she had felt before. Enchantment and necromancy, mind and darkness. Death.

The crystal's function and command unfolded before her sight. Its destructive power coursed through her, spread itself out before her like she might be watching a warrior's blade being forged, beaten, tempered, honed, and tempered again in a blur of compressed time.

When it was done, Elathien was pale and shaking. She felt her stomach heave, vomiting forth a measure of wine conspicuously free of the pearl dust that the magic threading her body had consumed. She washed the taste away with more wine. She encased the shard carefully in its sheath of lead, then wrapped that sheath in cloth before she returned it to her belt pouch.

She knew what the shard was now. But she had absolutely no idea what that knowledge meant.

She needed to get outside, needed to feel the air of the city. The closeness of her flat was suddenly stifling to her. Thaelind Heights was waiting, offering a distraction she needed right now. She woke Diranta, unceremoniously tapping him with her toe where he slumbered by the fire.

"Do you fancy a night out?" she said.

— SEVEN —

THE NIGHT WAS APPROACHING the point of dangerous lateness for those parts of Yewnyr not already dangerous from the first moment of the setting sun. However, the streets of upscale Thaelind Heights were as safe as anywhere else on the Ridge, toward which Elathien and Diranta hurtled now in the back of a coach cab.

The bright lights of that mountainside and its wards marked the homes and estates of Yewnyr's wealthier nobles and merchants, guildmasters and artists, criminals and adventurers. Elathien's family had always dwelled on the Ridge. However, it had been a long while since she'd found herself on the twisting course of Genslin Street where it marked the unofficial entry to the mountainside's steep switchback slopes.

The hansom driver was one she had used before for his exhaustive knowledge of the Free City, Elathien confirming as they set out that "house of fourteen lights" gave no hint of an address or location in Thaelind he recognized. So she paid him to take her on a lengthy tour of the ward, remembering landmarks and noting activity on the street as she passed. This wasn't her family's domain, their estate higher up in both location and standing in Edalithien House Ward. But even then, she felt the tug of faint but familiar memories from childhood, of noble's galas and coming-of-age dances tucked away in the shadows of Thaelind's now-icy streets.

Along one of those streets, the cab twice passed a sentry in the uniform of a private militia walking a patrol through the shadows. A high wall and the bare branches of an arboretum loomed behind him, as did the lights of a gatehouse a short distance away. Through the frost-screened side window, Elathien caught him watching the cab the second time they passed, so she called to the driver to stop a dozen strides beyond him.

As the cab rolled to a halt, Elathien assessed the young Human and judged him as good a place as any to start with first inquiries. She recognized the uniform of the private company called the Silver Blades. They worked exclusively in Thaelind Heights, and the stars of a sergeant at his shoulder suggested that he'd been on the job in the ward for a while now.

Elathien pulled opened the window, raising her voice a tone above its normal register as she called back to the patrol sergeant where he watched the cab. "If it please you, sir," she said, "could a stranger to Thaelind ask a question of you?"

By his height and the unruly beard, the sergeant might have had twenty-five summers on him. By the look on his face when he drew close enough to Elathien, he was younger in spirit than in body. She leaned through the window, draping bodice and breasts over the frame to provide an unparalleled view at exactly eye level as he approached.

"Thank you, sir. I fear that I am both late and lost. I would be forever grateful for directions from one who knows the ward."

Before setting out, Elathien had changed into garb suitable for a noble's night out, the bodice tied tightly over lace and a sheath of silk blouse. She wore sweeping black skirts and a blood-red sash that concealed the scabbard belt for the single long-knife at her back. That knife was hidden beneath the cloak edged in rabbit that was draped across her, hanging so as to hide the tattoos that traced from her shoulders and down her back, but not obscuring the bodice's wide-open front and what lay within. The frigid air had her almost painfully erect, nipples visible through all three layers of cloth. The sergeant's eyes were drawn to her hardness, and to the pale globes those upthrust points marked out.

"Of course, my lady," he stammered. "Where is it you seek?"

"Oh, please, sir. My mother is 'my lady'." Elathien spoke in quiet tones, forcing him to step closer to hear her. "You may call me Dacani."

"Of course, my lady. Mistress Dacani, I mean to say. What house do you seek?"

"Well, I'm afraid that's the difficulty, or my driver should surely have found it by now. A gentleman friend of mine is a lover of riddles, I'm afraid, and bade me look for him tonight in Thaelind Heights at the house of fourteen lights. I assumed it would mean some landmark easily recognized, but his wit is clearly greater than mine."

"I don't know that that's any address, mistress. But I've heard tell that the Fourteen Lights is a militia operating out of Chaede Street. Perhaps your gentleman friend meant for you to ask of them for directions, my lady. Mistress, I mean to say."

With a speed the sergeant never could have anticipated, Elathien shot a hand out to his neck, pulling him forward for a perfunctory kiss of thanks on the forehead. She felt his gasp of breath warm in the shadow between her breasts. She made sure she had smoothed away her smile when she let him stumble back.

With a wave, she slid the window shut and tapped to the driver. Where she glanced back, she saw the sergeant absently adjusting the set of his breeches. Elathien smiled again as the cab raced on into the night.

Chaede Street was easy enough to find, and Elathien had the driver make a slow pass along it as she carefully scanned the buildings to both sides. The private militias of Yewnyr were too many to count, and came and went with the fortunes of the families and mercantile concerns that bankrolled them. Still, the fact that Elathien couldn't recall even having heard of the Fourteen Lights made her wary.

It took three more stops across the ward to narrow the search, all of them made at well-lit taverns where she happily let the eyes of barkeep and patrons roam across her as she repeated the same story she had used for the sergeant. Elathien kept her cloak as loose as the cold allowed, holding the dog firmly on a leash that he abhorred, but which he put up with at her request. To any casual glance, she was a woman of means, secure in the protection of the black watchdog that strutted at her heels.

It was the last tavern, a house called the Dancing Spirits, where she found what she needed. Somewhat ironically, it came courtesy of a barmaid whose dispassionate expression told Elathien she was immune to her charms.

"Baine House," the barmaid said. "Black stone facade with a gate of vines, two blocks back. The Fourteen Lights have guest-house apartments there that they watch over. Don't tell them you heard it here, though."

"Of course not," Elathien said. "And thank you so much."

As she and Diranta swept out, she heard the barmaid call to her. "You ask me, your gentleman friend's making things too complicated for his own good."

"Indeed," Elathien replied as she slipped back to the street.

The dark stones of Baine House were flecked with frost, gleaming with the light of the waning-full Clearmoon as it crested the adjacent skyline, free now of the day's cloud. Elathien had the hansom driver swing past only once, not wanting to risk a return in case anyone was watching. She scanned the windows as she passed, counting lights in three lower apartments but noting the upper floor dark. The wrought-iron gate in the shape of climbing vines was dark as well, marking the fact that any-one prone to passing that way by night would have an escort.

Elathien signaled the cab to stop a safe distance around the corner, midway back to the Dancing Spirits so that the tavern would provide a reasonable place to be walking to or from if anyone asked. She and Diranta stepped out with a nod to the driver, who was bringing up wa-ter and blankets from beneath his seat for the horses. Not knowing how long it would take, Elathien had paid him well and in advance for a night's worth of his time.

As she approached, she noted that Baine House wasn't identified as such anywhere on its facade. No name or number. Not even a sign to mark the narrow alleyway that was the access to its stairs. If not for the barmaid, there would have been no way to even connect the site to Ne-rani's description. Even in a part of the city that took security seriously, this was a place that existed only for those who already knew how to find it.

The gate had no lock, as was the norm with such places. No incon-venience to the approach of those who had business here, and a subtle warning to those who didn't that the real security lay beyond. The stairs from the narrow lane were as difficult to find in the dark as they were to climb, twisting up and around at an angle that hid them from casual observation. Elathien counted the doors along the way as the floors she had seen from the street, stopping at the last whose windows had been dark. As good a place as any to start. She would end up speaking to the folk behind the doors below her, she expected, but a short while prowl-ing an empty flat for a sense of who lived here could help shape her questions.

She listened carefully at the door, catching no sound from beyond. The stairs behind her were equally silent. The lock was well built but no match for Elathien's picks, which she carried hidden in a thigh sheath. A few moments spent in concentration, then she felt the tumblers shift. She took a moment to detect for dweomer but the door was clear.

Diranta entered ahead of her, listening, but the rooms beyond the foyer were as silent as they were dark. The air was freezing, the dank scent of mold noticeable but not oppressive. The stove in the kitchen was well made, but it had been some time since these chambers had felt the heat of a fire.

Except that in a building like this, in a ward like Thaelind, apart-ments didn't stay empty long enough for even the faint hint of decay to set in. Particularly places watched over by a militia's private security. Elathien felt herself on edge suddenly. She reached beneath her cloak absently, loosening the long-knife in its scabbard.

The shadows of shelves and high-backed chairs loomed in a sitting room to her right as she entered, a kitchen to the left whose glass doors to the balcony beyond were etched with frost. Through the sitting room, she spied an open door to the bedchamber, moon's-light gleaming through a white-streaked window to show a tangled mass of quilts spilled down to the floor.

The cantrip of detection was still active as Elathien carefully paced the sitting room, but she felt no trace of dweomer in the place. She let the spell fade from her mind to bring up magical light instead, touching the glass shield of a lamp on a side table to set it glowing daylight bright. She carried it as she inspected both rooms, as well as the bath and toilet off the kitchen.

The furniture in the sitting room was sturdy but plain, which put it most out of place with the style of the neighborhood. The shelves of both kitchen and sitting room were sparsely stocked. Well-used dishes. Wooden and pewter tableware. A basket of frost-furred and blackened fruit. A few bound volumes of poetry stood out among news journals and broadsheets stacked in piles, none of them more recent than two months past.

The bedchamber held a four-poster bed set with horsehair mattress beneath a thin featherbed. The quilts were good quality and well stained. Two dark robes of heavy wool were laid across the room's single chair. Elathien snapped her fingers to call Diranta back where he attempted to sniff them.

Stepping close to the bed, she could see well-worn grooves at the narrowest part of each bedpost's crown. In the bottom of a narrow wardrobe, she found the looped leather thongs that had made the marks. No need to guess as to their function and purpose.

A half-dozen long women's shifts in light cotton hung in the wardrobe as well, all dirty, all pushed far to the left to leave half the space empty. Elathien scanned the interior carefully in the light of the lamp. Then she moved the shifts across on their narrow iron bar, revealing the side panel they had clumsily hidden.

She didn't need to search long to find where a slice of paneling had been forced out of its groove, then replaced. The width of her hand, it moved only with effort, but the light caught the narrow gap it revealed in the wardrobe's base. Something was wrapped there in a skin of dark rags, Elathien whispering the incantation of detection by instinct. Within the unseen field that she shaped with mind and cantrip, she felt a dweomer of magic flare.

Carefully, she unwrapped the small bundle to reveal a talisman in gleaming steel. A plain disc scribed with arcane runes, it was punched with two holes along one edge, through which a leather thong was threaded. The weave of the talisman's dweomer was familiar to her mind. Conjuration and the magic of movement. Teleportation most likely, but its specifics were a blank to her. She would need to spend some time to ascertain its power, and to guess at why it might be hidden here.

In the doorway behind her, Diranta gave a low growl.

Elathien flashed the dog a finger sign that quieted him as she stepped back into the sitting room with the lamp held high, ready to quell its magical light with a word.

The figure standing in the open space where the sitting room met the foyer was a broad-shouldered Essaruk whose grey cloak showed the lines of at least two weapons. Elathien saw him appraising her appearance openly, eyes lingering at her bodice. She fought the urge to furl her cloak closed around her, letting him leer for the distraction it offered. His grey-brown complexion fairly gleamed in Elathien's light, his tone impassive as he spoke.

"You are in ten different kinds of trouble, mistress." He had the carefully paced accent of the east, the Essaruk kingdoms of Daegraleth across the Leagin Sea. Most of the Essaruk in Yewnyr were of the Scattered Kingdoms and the northlands, their accent a harsh hybrid of Norgyr and their own guttural tongue.

"Is that so?" she said evenly.

He pushed the cloak back to reveal a warrior's body under chainshirt and a black leather kilt. A set of truncheons hung at his belt, thick shafts of ironwood studded with blunted nails. Diranta growled again but Elathien signaled him to the floor, the dog dropping without hesitation. Though she knew how quickly a second signal would have him up and at the Essaruk's throat, she wanted the stranger off his guard. He didn't take his eyes from her in any event.

From the inside pocket of her cloak where she had already secured the talisman, Elathien carefully pulled the wallet with her credentials and cards. With a carefree gesture, she tossed it to the silent figure. He snatched it from the air, glancing to it quickly enough that she knew he recognized its interlocking seals as genuine.

The Essaruk smiled the disturbing grin of his kind, teeth gleaming, lips bared to reveal his spiked incisors. "Impressive. Also, in giving to me, not so smart." He kept the wallet in hand as he pulled one of the truncheons free with the other. "You are going to tell me what you are doing here. And I hope before nothing bad happens, hey?"

"If 'bad' includes me shoving both those walking sticks down your throat and out your ass, I'd call it unlikely."

"Ah, you like to talk tough, hey? You know something I don't?"

The Essaruk took a step toward her. Elathien sensed Diranta tense up, but true to his training, the dog didn't move.

"I know that I just spoke a description of you to the operative I have waiting at the other end of this, back at the Dancing Spirits." Elathien held up the cracked black gemstone where she had slipped it from her belt pouch as she left the bedchamber. "Also, I know that when I tell him to move, he'll have a City Watch patrol with him when he gets here on the run. That's two things I know that you don't, but I'm not sure we have time to list everything."

Despite its dweomer, the stone gave no outward appearance of magic as some items did. Elathien made sure to hold it at an angle where the lamp would catch it, throwing up a corona of black light. She saw the Essaruk's eyes narrow, his expression telling her that even if he didn't recognize the stone of sending for what it was, he at least half-believed what it could be.

"I apologize if my tone gave offense," he growled. He offered the disturbing smile again, his tone showing a maximum amount of grudging deference.

Elathien didn't bother telling the Essaruk that she was likely to be in more trouble than he was if the watch actually did show up. The gemstone, the red-black crystal in the pouch of her belt, and the newly found talisman were all lacking the arcane bond needed to carry them legally. Possession of restricted magic in Yewnyr was one of the most straightforward routes to a sentence on the work gangs — a fact Elathien knew from dark experience and had no intention of learning again.

"I'm sure you do." She made sure that the Essaruk saw the stone stay in her hand. "You know my name," she said, nodding to her credentials. "How about you return the favor?" She caught the wallet as it was thrown back.

"Call me Cahlad. I serve to deliver private investigation skills and security. No doubt so much like yourself. You will tell me, please, how you are here?"

"I'm here because I broke in. If you can't figure that out, your investigation skills need work. Now you can tell me what you're doing here, starting with what happened to the girl. Irandis."

It was nothing more than a guess at this point that the dead girl had been here. But too many things felt wrong about the flat, starting with its state of empty abandonment, and ending with the Essaruk's sudden appearance that told Elathien the site was being watched.

The truth was the only thing she had to work with at this point, and the Essaruk's moment of hesitation in reaction to it told her she'd guessed right.

"You know Irandis?" Cahlad said evenly. "You tell her to come home. The city is cold, she could get hurt."

Elathien paced slowly into the sitting room, making sure to stay back of the line between the Essaruk and Diranta where the dog still lay, watching. "She did get hurt. She's dead nine days."

Cahlad gave her a smirk, but it was hard to read. The Essaruk mouth with its thrusting canine teeth didn't lend itself to subtle emotion.

"I am sorry to hear that. And I apologize for our introduction again." He shrugged as he set the truncheon back to his belt. "Irandis went missing, I assumed she fell in with bad folk. I think you are them, I react."

"I admire your dedication." Elathien set the lamp down on the side table it had come from, pacing past it and into shadow so that Cahlad couldn't see her slip a long-knife from its scabbard. She kept it in hand, under her cloak and behind her. "What can you tell me about Irandis?"

"What can you tell me? How did she die?"

"An accident, in the healing refuge where she was staying." She watched carefully for any sign of recognition in the Essaruk, but his expression was a thoughtful blank. "Your turn."

Cahlad sighed with what Elathien thought was just a little too much care. "I am private security for certain well-connected families of Yewnyr," he said.

"Fourteen Lights." The Essaruk's eyes narrowed like he wasn't happy that Elathien knew the name, but he nodded.

"I like my job, mostly," he said. "Keeping track of family, arranging guards for travel, those things. One part I do not like is keeping secret the… indiscretions of my employers. Most unpleasant."

Elathien recognized the look in his eye. He was working with the truth for the same reason she was, hoping to judge her reaction. Seeing how much of the story she already knew. She felt something in her stomach tighten, but she kept that feeling from the blank mask of her face.

"It is important," Cahlad said. "This conversation between us, it does not happen, hey?"

"That depends on who your employers are."

"I don't tell you their names, because you know their names. Nobles of the Ridge. Members of the council of city lords, some of them. Important people, big secrets."

"And Irandis…"

"One of those secrets. Indiscretions."

Elathien had to push the image of the leather thongs, the gouges on the bedposts from her mind. "How long was this going on?"

"Since years."

"Since Irandis was a child."

Cahlad smiled the unreadable smile again. "As I say. Most unpleasant. I do not know much about Irandis. Where she comes from, how she comes here. But she is fragile, yes? Something not right in her."

"I can't imagine why."

Cahlad shrugged. "She is kept here, she is kept safe. But a month past, she disappears. I have rooms downstairs. I hear you inside here, I hope you are her. You are not, I worry you are who took her. Again, my apologies…"

"While Irandis was here, do you know if she ever spoke of a sister? She might have been like Irandis. Fragile."

"Nothing said to me. She has no family, she says. When she went missing, no one to look for her."

Elathien felt something at her fingers suddenly. Diranta had risen against her order, nuzzling her with a low whine that made her realize her hand was shaking. She tried to fight it, but something in Cahlad's words had triggered emotions she still had so little control over.

"Are you all right, mistress?" the Essaruk said, but Elathien swung wide around him as she made for the open door.

She summoned up all the composure left in her to say, "We're done here." She nodded formally to back up the sentiment, sheathing the knife as she went and not caring that Cahlad could see.

She stumbled twice on the dark stairs, but managed to steady herself by the time she reached the gate and its frosted vines. With Diranta at her heel, she walked stolidly, eyes cold as she made her way back to the hansom. She kept her footfalls to near silence, listening for any sense or sound of Cahlad following. The street stayed empty behind her, though, even with a glance back as she approached the hansom and motioned the driver to prepare to go.

Only when she was within the cab and the horses were moving for home did she let the emotion take her, crying quietly for the sake of the things she knew now about Irandis. For the sake of other things she couldn't forget, and which would overwhelm her at times with no rhyme or reason.

When she went missing, no one to look for her.

Diranta set his head in her lap as she slipped from the bench to the floor of the cab. His neck was warm against her arms as she held him tight.

The hansom was down the slopes of the Ridge and halfway to the bridges when Elathien tapped to signal the driver. He slid the window with a nod, Elathien carefully wiping her eyes as she gave him a change of destination. "Brarfeld Ward." South of the river, past Mirayth Ward and Blackheath standing dark in the night. "Elor Street," she said, the address of Cirhela's flat pulled from her memory for the first time in nine months as the cab sped on.

The skeptical porter at the gated white-stone apartment block was no one she remembered from before. He called up only at Elathien's repeated insistence, keeping one eye on Diranta as he made his way up the spiral stairs. When he returned, Cirhela was two steps behind him.

The healer didn't speak as she ushered Elathien in. Just embraced her with wide-open arms, wiping the tears away. She was arrayed for bed, a robe of light cotton over a shift and leggings in white. She draped an arm around Elathien as she led her and Diranta past the porter and up the stairs, his gaze following them as they climbed.

By the time they were out of sight of that gaze, Cirhela's hand was beneath Elathien's cloak, tentative. Questioning. In answer, Elathien slipped her own hand inside the healer's shift, feeling the warmth of bare breast beneath even before Cirhela's door had opened.

When that door closed, Elathien was pushed back against it as the healer embraced her, their lips touching softly. The muted candlelight, the scent of the flat filled her with the feeling of having come home — a sensation that she suddenly realized how much she missed. She reached up, entangling her hands in Cirhela's dark hair to return that first kiss in full, feeling time slow as the healer's sigh filled her.

When Elathien finally drew breath again, Cirhela was staring deep into her eyes. So many things hung unsaid between them, the healer's passion a thing that Elathien could feel. Her own emotions were more difficult to read.

"Are you all right?" Cirhela said at last, wiping one last tear from Elathien's cheek with her fingers. "Would you like a drink?" She led her by the hand into the spacious sitting room, a fire burning down in the river-rock fireplace that dominated the far wall. Elathien shook her head as she sat on an overstuffed settee, Cirhela walking to the sideboard to pour a goblet of red for herself.

Elathien realized she was staring longingly at the healer's full lips as she sat. Cirhela took a sip of wine and leaned in to gently kiss her again, but Elathien responded hungrily, sucking the wine from her lips, her forehead pressed to the healer's, eyes closed.

"Take me…" Elathien whispered.

They made it down the short hall to the bedchamber with arms and tongues entwined, stumbling through the open door. The room was sparse, as Elathien remembered it. Lace pillows, a full-length mirror, framed cameos of long-lost relatives above a carved wooden bedstead. "I've missed you," she whispered. "I'm sorry…"

But Cirhela cut her off with her mouth, her tongue drawing the words out to a lingering gasp. Then the noble's robe Elathien wore, the shift, the cloak, the silk and lace and scabbard beneath it were all off, and they were falling back to let the bed embrace them both.

In the front foyer, Diranta had laid himself down before the door. He cocked his head more than once at the sounds issuing from the distant shadows before he finally let himself sleep.

— EIGHT —

IT WAS STILL DARK outside when Elathien fled Cirhela's flat, carefully extricating herself from a tangle of blankets and limbs. The dark-haired healer had seemingly enveloped her while she slept, one leg across Elathien's as if subliminally trying to anchor her there, one hand cupping the softness of her sex. The healer's head was resting on her breast, Elathien shifting with great care as she listened for any change in the sound of her gentle breathing.

Finally free, she lingered a moment longer before slipping from the bed to pad naked to the wardrobe. She set a soundless charm around her as she rifled its rails and drawers for clothing that might fit her, conscious of the difference between her and Cirhela in size. In the end, she selected leggings that would tuck safely into her boots, and a tunic of dark wool whose extra length would almost look like a match to a style fashionable a few winters back. With the cloak she also borrowed, the ensemble would at least get her through the streets with less notice than her noble's outfit of the night before.

She carefully picked that outfit up where it lay scattered between the bed and the chamber door, bundling it as she laid the new clothes out. Despite her best efforts, she remembered far too vividly the process of having left it there. She couldn't remember Cirhela disrobing, though, conscious only of the moment when the healer's body was against hers, breast to breast, belly to belly, mouth to mouth. Cirhela's strong embrace pinned her at the shoulder as her other hand traced down her back and across her buttocks, pulling her close. Elathien's eyes were half-shut, her hands mounding Cirhela's full breasts when she felt the healer push her suddenly back, forcing her down onto the soft green duvet.

Cirhela had started by draping herself across her, caressing Elathien body to body as she rained kisses down on her neck, her shoulders, her aching breasts. She could do little more than gasp, the duvet bunching in her hands. Then with a smile that Elathien remembered only too well, Cirhela raised her legs, then slowly lowered her head to taste and drink her wetness.

The healer's skill with her tongue was beyond compare, as was the need that Elathien felt in that tongue's embrace. Her own hunger over-

— 61 —

took her too quickly, and with no warning, her pleasure had peaked and burst and peaked again like a pent-up storm. She could only lay there, moaning as Cirhela crawled up the bed to lie beside her, Elathien reaching for her, cupping her face in her hands as she kissed her deeply, tasting the musk of her own sex on the healer's lips. Cirhela's hands trembled as they caressed their way along her body again, and Elathien felt a passion, a wholeness, a contentment that she hadn't felt in so long.

She forced herself up and over, pinning Cirhela as she hungrily took her ample breasts in her mouth. The healer's nipples were nut-brown and rigid with desire, Elathien's tongue tasting each in turn as her hands reacquainted themselves with the curve of her belly and thighs. One of those hands settled in at last on Cirhela's neatly trimmed sex, the healer spreading her legs slowly as Elathien's fingers sought out her wetness and the pink pearl that nestled within.

Cirhela's climax came fast and strong, but that only increased Elathien's hunger as she swung around on the bed, fingers tracing across the healer's body as she settled in backwards on top of her. Then the two of them had cried out together over what seemed like the whole of the night, as the conjoined tremor that Elathien remembered passed through them again and again. The sound of that passion, the feel and taste of it, the sensation of the healer's tongue at her sex, her hands in her hair — all the things she had forced from her mind nine months ago, just as she forced them from her mind now while she finished dressing.

Diranta was still waiting for her in the foyer where he had spent the night. Elathien moved close to keep the sudden thump of his wagging tail within her dweomer of silence. She sighted down the short corridor to see Cirhela still asleep before she slipped out and away.

It was a short hike to the dark-frosted streets of Mirayth from Brarfeld's bright apartment blocks, visible behind Elathien as she walked along the slight rise that lifted the ward above the river lowlands to the north. She walked directly from Cirhela's to the gates of Blackheath, forgetting until she sighted the refuge's grey walls that the silver sigil badge Cirhela had provided her was back in her own flat.

She didn't doubt her ability to talk her way through the front gates in short order. However, she knew that any such attempt would be the first thing Cirhela heard of when she arrived herself, and Elathien was acutely conscious suddenly of not wanting the healer to come looking for her. Not yet.

In the end, she led Diranta along the narrow lanes that wrapped around Blackheath, slipping through the chill shadow of the closest apartments where they rose above. The refuge's kitchen doors were locked, but not well enough to keep her out. In the cluttered storage corridor beyond, no sentries questioned or halted her as she slipped through. But that was odd, Elathien thought, remembering Cirhela talking about how the Masters of Administration had undertaken additional security in the aftermath of Nerani wandering into the refuge unchallenged.

The Masters of Administration meant Lady Dacani. Elathien filed the thought away.

A sigil badge she borrowed from a cloak hung outside the toilets carried her from the kitchens, through a network of storerooms, past the laundry, and into the mezzanine. Diranta at her heel got more than his fair share of questioning looks as Elathien took the stairs to the Administration Tower. However, she knew from experience that looking as though you were sure of your destination would keep all but the most perceptive and curious from wondering where you were going.

Her first goal in the Blackheath records rooms was to get a quick look at the Master's schedules to ensure that Cirhela's work for the day wasn't bringing her anywhere near the records rooms. Satisfied that this was the case, Elathien then settled in to address her second goal. She needed to discover as much as she could regarding Magister Sirnos, trying to get a sense of his work and magic, and of any disruption to the patterns of that work in the days before his grisly end. In those patterns, she hoped and expected that she would discover more about the time Irandis and Nerani had spent at Blackheath, and the connection to Magister Sirnos that she knew instinctively was there.

Nothing was better for blurring the passage of time than the stale scent of dusty paper and the repetitive tone of official records. And so it was that Elathien passed the day away in what seemed like a relative heartbeat. She was alone for most it, setting herself up at a quiet corner table with Diranta at her feet. Away from the windows and out of sight of the doors, she read by the light of a half-shrouded evenlamp, only the occasional clerk or healer passing within line of sight.

A few of those looked like they were intent on questioning her presence there. Elathien deflected most with a look of dark impatience, and by the conspicuous presentation of her investigator's credentials and stolen badge among the papers and scrolls she sorted through. The one who actually spoke to her, a sour scribe struggling with a stack of leather-bound records as he passed, she sent on his way by telling him that she was there on instructions from Lady Dacani, and guessing from his reaction that he had no intention of confirming that.

From the room's tall cabinets and dusty shelves, she pulled an exactingly complete public history of Magister Sirnos's time at Blackheath. All of it was there — his research, his studies, his notes and recommendations for the hundreds of convalescents who had passed within his purview over long years. Then when she needed to break the tedium of digging through that history, Elathien spent time with the steel talisman she had stolen from the wardrobe in the Thaelind Heights flat.

Like the blood-red crystal shard, this too would have bent to the efforts of the divination of identity, revealing its function and secrets to Elathien's magic. However, the pearls she would have required for that spell were back at her flat, forcing her to focus on a lesser understanding.

Carefully, while the cantrip of detection filled her, Elathien felt and tested the edges of the talisman's dweomer with her mind. Through careful probing, she sensed the magical foundations of its power, even if the specifics weren't clear. The disc offered up some manner of teleportation to its wielder, but how far-reaching or with what restrictions, she had no way of knowing. Its level of power suggested potent spellcraft, however.

It was growing dark outside when she stood to stretch at the battered oak table. The number of bound records and folio pages spread across it had grown steadily all day. However, despite the number of pages she had read, the files she had sorted through, she had made no notes of her own.

"When you talked last night, you said you'd tell me more in the morning."

Elathien started, turning to see Cirhela approaching from the direction of the closest door. The white walls behind her were mottled in red-black shadow, a trace of sunset forcing itself in at the distant windows.

"Sorry," was all Elathien could think to say. She hadn't heard the door open, hadn't seen Diranta stand to quietly warn her. She was more tired than she realized.

"What you said last night. What you discovered. It's true?"

Elathien nodded. The conversation had come in the exhausted aftermath of their pleasure, Cirhela holding her tightly as she haltingly told the story. "Irandis was held for fate knows how long as a noble's plaything in Thaelind Heights. A sex slave from the time she was a child. Yes, it's true."

Cirhela stepped up to the table. She glanced down at the scattered files, not so much because she was interested, Elathien guessed, but because the healer didn't want to show her reaction.

"I met someone who said he knew her," Elathien said, continuing with the story she had managed to impart the previous night before Cirhela forced her to stop talking. "A private security operative. Her handler, I expect. The way he described Irandis, the things that likely happened to her, would seem to point to her ending up in Blackheath as a result of that trauma." From the table before her, Cirhela opened up a folded sheet of heavy folio paper. It was marked with the same sigils and notices that protected all the convalescent files of Blackheath. Nerani's files, and Irandis's.

"She was found wandering in Anduras Hamlets," Cirhela said quietly.

"She might have been on the streets for a while then. Wandering down from the Ridge."

"And what about Nerani?"

"Cahlad, the operative, said he didn't know her. I judged it as the truth, for whatever that's worth." Elathien gauged the level of pain in Cirhela's look as the healer opened Irandis's file. "I'm sorry," she said. "I know you cared about the girl."

"I did," Cirhela said. "And that explains my reaction, certainly. You're the one I'm more worried about."

"I'm fine," Elathien said evenly.

Cirhela let the file drop as she stepped closer, tucking a strand of Elathien's auburn hair back behind her ear. "That's not the picture you presented last night," she said. "That's not why you came to me, then left in the middle of the night without a word."

A half-dozen different lies slipped through Elathien's mind in reaction to the question left hanging by Cirhela's concern. She ignored them all as she pulled the wrapped bundle from her belt pouch. She opened it carefully and unsealed the lead foil, noting the faint trembling at her fingers. Set out on the cloth where she spread it along the edge of the table, the blood-red crystal shard flared within a dark corona as it caught the evenlamp's pale light.

"Did you do your reading? You know what it is?"

"Powerful," Elathien said, and she remembered how shaken the divination from the previous night had left her. "Enchantment and necromancy magic, constrained by dark commands. By my understanding, the enchantment weaves spells of charming and control on the mind of a victim, wiping clear that mind and its memories at the level of thought. Then the crystal's necromantic power burns out the physical mind in that blank state, destroying what's been cleared. That's what divination tells me, at any rate. The only way to find out more would be to use it."

"Magister Sirnos…" Cirhela's voice carried a current of rage where she stared, the red-black light of the crystal fading as her trembling hand moved closer to it. "You said you found this in his offices. I cannot believe he would have possessed such a thing."

"He possessed three of them by my count. This was the only one remaining."

Elathien saw Cirhela make the moonsign against evil. A subtle motion of two fingers marked out twin crescent shapes across her breast, an odd thing to see in one whose own craft and knowledge of magic should have put her above such superstitions.

"You don't think…" The healer was on edge, having trouble finding the words. "Could this magic have been what happened to Irandis? To Nerani?"

"I wondered that myself," Elathien said. "Except that everything I learned last night, everything I saw, tells me that Irandis's mind was likely broken by the life she lived. The hurt she bore was more than enough. There would have been no need to hurt her any other way."

Cirhela stepped away from the table, Elathien seeing how drawn she looked. How very weary. She fought the urge to go to the healer's side, the vulnerability of the night before still rooting deep inside her. She knew what road it would lead her down if she let it.

"To use such magic against a sentient creature is the definition of evil," Cirhela said. "Why would you assume that such evil would conform to any sense or logic?"

"Because even evil takes the path of least resistance when it can. Assume Magister Sirnos used the crystal. Or assume he was simply holding it for another capable of that level of violence. The timing makes no sense. Both Irandis and Nerani were clearly ill before they were brought to Blackheath. You said so yourself. But if someone at Blackheath was responsible for creating that illness, why bring either girl to the one place with the best chance of curing it? The best chance of revealing that complicity?"

Cirhela could only nod as Elathien sealed the crystal into its sheath of lead, wrapping it and slipping it once more to her belt. "There would be no cure for this," the healer said quietly. "A disenchantment might unravel some of the effect of the charm, but it would do nothing to affect the physical damage to brain and mind. The most powerful healing could undo all but the most grievous wounding of the mind, but would leave that healed mind in the blank state etched upon it by the charm."

Where Elathien was sorting through her notes at the table, she was surprised suddenly to find Cirhela's hand on hers. "When you learned this last night," the healer said. "I can understand how it might have affected you.

"Yes." The warmth of Cirhela's touch reminded Elathien suddenly that she was cold.

"But that's not why you came to me last night."

"No."

"You're still hurting, Elathien."

"When she spoke last night," Elathien said, "Nerani said that Irandis knew names." She shifted her hand away from Cirhela's as she slipped loose records and notes back to the proper folios. Her mind had tracked the movement of every page as she worked, now reversing the patterns it had laid down to replace everything where she had found it. "*Irandis knew what they did,* Nerani said. She knew how they lied."

Cirhela accepted Elathien's change of subject with a trace of reluctance. "What do you think that means? And how does it connect to Magister Sirnos's death?"

"It absolutely doesn't connect. I've gone through every convalescent file and daily schedule in Sirnos's files for the past two months. All the records show that he never even met Irandis before she died."

"So you think Laicos was right? There's nothing here?"

"I might. Except that the records are missing something."

From the pouch of her belt, Elathien drew forth the note found in the magister's desk, as well as the near-identical note that Cirhela herself had given her. She unfolded them both. She saw the healer stare, not understanding.

"A copy of Nerani's note? From where?"

"From five weeks ago," Elathien said. "And from Magister Sirnos's office. And it's not Nerani's note. Irandis wrote this."

She turned the paper over, revealing the date, Irandis's name, and the magister's signature that she had seen in the office as Lady Dacani burst in. *This notation recorded by my hand on this date, and entered into record.* It was a standard bit of wording that accompanied any documents making up part of a convalescent's assessment. The note that Nerani had written carried the same wording, but the name on that paper was Cirhela's own.

"I never..." The healer was flustered. "I don't know this note."

"You wouldn't have had a chance to, with Sirnos hiding it. But look at this."

From beneath the files spread across the closest corner of the desk, Elathien pulled another sheet of well-folded paper. Lines of erratic script filled the page in charcoal pencil, the writing barely legible in places.

"I would like to dwell in a garden," Elathien read. "I would like to dwell in green places where the walls cannot hold me. I would like to see the sun again before I go."

"That was Nerani a week ago," Cirhela said. "When she was first found. An initial assessment of her literacy and mental focus, a standard procedure." The healer turned the paper over, showing her own name and the familiar notation there.

"But the handwriting is different. Look. There's no overt likeness between Nerani's script a week ago and her script two days before Sirnos was killed." Elathien laid the samples side by side, the two wholly dissimilar. The first was cramped. Uncertain and unsteady, like the thoughts that drove it were breaking even as the words were formed. The second was the angular script that spoke to a focus and power. *Words that carry such anger can hurt us,* Elathien remembered herself saying. "But that script two days past is a likeness for the handwriting of Nerani's dead sister."

"Identical..."

"Not precisely. It's close, though. And though I'm not an expert, if you want to bring one in, she'll tell you that the newer note is Nerani doing a well-practiced forgery."

"But why?"

Elathien began to sort papers back into the folders they'd come from. It was a question she'd been pondering most of the day herself, and she still wasn't as close to an answer as she wanted to be. "At a guess, to lend credence to the illusion that Irandis is still with her. Nerani had an old letter or diary. Words left to her. She learned to mimic the script from it so that the part of her subconscious that needs to be in contact with Irandis can have an outlet. Those words left to her might well be all she had."

"The words that Sirnos was hiding… This is more than chance, Elathien."

"No doubt. But if you're talking about a connection between Nerani and Irandis, the evidence doesn't hold. Not yet, at least."

"But twins have been known to carry mystical bonds," Cirhela said. "Sorcerous, animyst, druidic potential all runs in bloodlines."

"Or it doesn't. Everyone in my family looked on in horror the first time I manifested anything resembling magic."

"And your brother…"

Elathien couldn't tell whether Cirhela cut herself off by instinct or in reaction to the tension twisting through her suddenly. She didn't look at the healer as she lifted a stack of folders to be returned to their shelves.

"I've read of studies," Cirhela said, her tone cautious. "Experiments at the School of Shadow showed that twins with spellcasting potential can share detectable emotive communication in certain instances. Nonverbal links. Fear. Trauma. Pain."

"But how many of the subjects were deceased?" Elathien slotted folders back by memory. Though she had made careful notes during the interviews with the sentries and healers who were potential witnesses to Magister Sirnos's demise, she had learned long ago to never put her own thoughts into writing. Not setting anything down in a form that could be taken from her, used against her. She trusted now to a recall that told her how to place two folders that would have been identical to anyone else's eyes, noting faint differences in the creases that marked their edges.

"The pain of death creates a spike of animys that can be channeled by countless dark rituals," Cirhela said. "That's not a power that can be discounted."

"I would never discount it. I just don't see the evidence for it being active here." Elathien turned back for the last of the files but left the three papers on the table. "You're too close to it. So be objective. Tell me what you see."

Cirhela was silent a moment. She was staring at the two notes seemingly copied one from the other, placed together so that the angular script seemed to bleed from one page to the next in smooth lines.

"Nerani has suffered extreme trauma too deep for healing to reach," Cirhela said quietly. "She shows no physical scars, but this only points out the depth of the things that have cut her. At the center of that trauma now is the loss of her sister, which has created the idea that her sister was killed by some outside intent. Nerani might have been looking for Irandis her whole life, and when she finally finds her dead, she suffers an extraordinary crisis of denial. Then she recreates Irandis in her mind as a result."

"A good explanation," Elathien said. "Almost perfect." As the last of the folders were returned to the shelf, she twisted to free her spine of the effects of a long day of sitting. Without looking, she could feel Cirhela's eyes follow the curve of her back as she stretched.

"Except," Cirhela said, "it ignores the question of how Nerani knows so much about the life and death of a sister she had lost for so long. But you don't think that Nerani felt her sister's death. That the pain of that death is what brought her here."

"I don't," Elathien said. "But I know she feels that pain now, and I'm wondering how badly she wants others to feel it with her."

"But if that is true, why Magister Sirnos? If he saw Irandis, why is there no record of it?"

"I don't know. Not yet."

Elathien snapped her fingers to call Diranta to her. The dog stood and shook himself, but then he ignored Elathien to cross to Cirhela, his tail in motion as she smilingly stroked his neck.

"I've missed him," Cirhela said. Elathien was silent. "When Nerani said that Irandis knew what they did, you think she was talking about the people who hurt Irandis?"

"It seems like a safe guess. Just as it seems a safer guess that Sirnos must have known some of those people. Important, the handler called them." Elathien heard an edge of anger in her voice that she wasn't expecting.

She crossed to where Cirhela and Diranta were standing. She rubbed the dog's shoulders, then felt Cirhela's hand slip into hers as she knew it would. "Sometimes I think he misses you, too," Elathien said.

One of her first jobs after going freelance had been a private murder investigation in Thunbridge Ward. She was still with Cirhela then, only a few weeks after she'd left Blackheath for what was supposed to be the last time. The maid at an estate had died in her sleep, and her noble employer feared that his drunkard wife had done the deed in a fit of misplaced jealous rage. He hoped that the warrant of a sanctioned investigator would prove him wrong, keeping his wife safe from accusation when the Yewnyr Guard inevitably became involved.

Elathien had recreated the death scene to find traces of the poison that killed the maid still in a stolen bottle of port in the servants' quarters. She also found traces of the antitoxin that had been administered to her immediately after death, clearing the poison from her system so that it wouldn't register to cursory magical detection.

That detection had also registered traces of the magical draught on the noble's sleeve, spattered there when he administered it. He'd washed his hands of the poison at least.

The noble had laughed as he paid Elathien off and told her how he expected her silence, thanking her for accomplishing the secret task he had hired her for. When he later used the same technique to kill his wife and whichever of her numerous lovers he next found her with, he would know better how to conceal his guilt.

Elathien left him bloodied but still breathing before she called the Guard herself.

When it was done, she had found Diranta locked in the kitchens, still a puppy and unfed in the absence of anyone looking after him. One of the dead maid's tasks, apparently. She left her investigator's warrant, including the noble's confession, but both she and the dog were gone by the time the Guard arrived.

Cirhela kissing her cheek distracted her from the faint glimmer of memory. "You're still hurting, Elathien. You need someone."

Elathien felt something twist in her chest. "I'm done with healers."

"That's not what I meant."

She snapped her fingers again, calling Diranta to her as she moved for the door. "I'll be back in the morning," she said, but Cirhela wasn't looking at her. Just staring at the papers and their identical script on the table before her as Elathien turned away.

— NINE —

THE GREY CORRIDORS were brighter this night as Tajamynar made his patrol. A clear sky shed light through the corridor's high windows, the waning Clearmoon rising above adjacent rooftops. Long shadows slanted across the floor from each shimmering expanse of force and glass, the sentry making a point of stepping into the light as he moved. His footsteps were a faint echo against the stones, but he listened more carefully to that echo this night than he ever had before.

The death of the magister two nights previous was still hanging heavy on him, though he had almost managed to push the image of the shattered body from his mind. In the aftermath, he had spoken with the Guard patrol as instructed, telling them just enough to avoid any risk of interrogation by the adepts and their truth charms. He had stayed clear of the refuge during the day, arriving only just in time for his night watch, and keeping the leather thong of talismans and charms he now wore at his belt hidden beneath the uniform's dark green sash.

Those charms were magic he had purchased that afternoon from one of the many sorcerers doing illegal business in Thanasi Bazaar. Their power and provenance had been checked by a disgraced former caster of the Authority Arcane who owed him favors, confirming protection against evil, against curses and undeath, all of which were weighing heavy on Tajamynar's mind.

As always, he checked each door along the corridors in turn, but this night, he kept his gaze sweeping to all sides as he did. So it was that he had ample warning of the figure crouched in shadow at the corridor's far end. At the windows near the head of the stairs, a slender girl hid from the spill of moon's-light, one arm raised as if to protect her eyes as that light reached for her.

The sentry was wary, touching a dagger tucked in beneath his tunic. Another protection he had taken to wearing, and as forbidden by the refuge as the magical protections he clasped now beneath the sash.

"Name yourself," he said brusquely, but even as he did, Tajamynar knew that this was no healer passing through the wards. "You're out of bounds and after dark. Tell me where you're meant to be, then get there."

The figure didn't move. He took a half-dozen cautious steps closer.

As she lowered her arm to look upon him, he saw the pain in the girl's bright eyes. The copper of her hair was fringed with the silver of the Clearmoon, hanging to shroud her face. She stared as if her gaze was something that might seize what it touched, and under the weight of that gaze, Tajamynar took a step back, recognition in his eyes. Then he faltered, standing as if struck. Trembling.

In the deserted corridor, a wind began to rise.

Like a hand had seized him, the sentry was spun toward the nearest window, stumbling as if fighting his own movements. He opened his mouth as if to scream, but all that emerged was a choking rasp as the air was pulled from him.

The girl rose, shakily stepping toward him even as he was dragged closer to her, jerking to a halt. She reached down to his waist, running both hands along his belly and the length of the sash. The loop of charms and talismans turned to sudden fire against the sentry's flesh, but the sound of his scream was smothered also as he was lifted off his feet and slammed up against the window behind him.

The girl stepped back, eyes wide, clearly as terrified as the sentry was. The talismans, the dagger, and the silver badge of leaves that had come off Tajamynar's sash were in her hand. A shudder coursed through her, and as it did, the wind that twisted around the sentry now slammed him back against the field of force that shrouded the window. Its magic shimmered in protest, groaning like metal bent at a black-smith's anvil.

For a long moment, he was held there, a marionette on unseen strings. Convulsions wracked him as arcane force twisted through his body, hands clutching feebly at the surrounding walls as he was pulled back, then slammed against the shimmering field of force. The pain of that force twisted through him, his eyes wide, mouth set in a silent scream. He lurched back again, slammed forward face first. Then again, looking for all the world as if he was hurling himself against the win-dow with intent, even as the terror in his expression showed how his will had been taken from him.

He managed two words as his breath left him for the last time. Barely heard over the howling wind. "Forgive me…"

With a hissing shriek, the protective field of force bent beneath a force even greater. Moon's-light flared within the window's open space, shimmering like water as Tajamynar was slammed against the glass as it shattered, opening up around him like a cocoon of crystal knives. Flesh and fingers, the skin of his face, the grey tunic and leggings and the body beneath were all sectioned and unfolded from each other like the petals of some blood-red flower. Then what was left of the sentry was caught by the maelstrom and flensed in a cloud of red, driven out to the freezing air. Falling in a sluice of flesh and bone to the ground far below.

In the corridor, the wind was gone, as was the girl where she stood in the shadows. No sound of footsteps marked her departure, no sign to be seen of how she had vanished into the night.

It was the Yewnyr Guard who woke Elathien this time before dawn, with a gruff apology and word to accompany them to Blackheath. She was still tired to her core, having fought most of the short night with dark dreams that fled with the pounding on her door and Diranta's growl in answer. Upon hearing the greeting, Elathien had been immediately afraid for Cirhela above all else. The dour Dwarf constable who attended her set her mind at ease, however, saying that it was Master Cirhela who had sent for her.

"She's sitting now for questioning in this affair," he said as they swept along the street, guards with evenlamps held aloft walking fast in front and back of them. Diranta was jogging at Elathien's side, despite the guard constable's initial protests at the dog accompanying her. "Investigator Laicos is with her."

"And what affair are we talking about? What's happened tonight?"

"Investigator Sergeant Laicos will answer all your questions, mistress."

"I doubt that very much," Elathien said, but if the constable heard her, he made no reply.

The sky above Blackheath's towers was still dark as they entered the great gates, faint streaks of sunlight making their first mark across dark cloud and a steel-hued night. The Guard were in evidence on all floors as Elathien was led up, past the Blackheath sentries standing darkly sullen behind them.

Approaching the head of the stairs, she recognized the shattered window even at a distance. Its adjacent panes were a clear shimmer in stark contrast to its spiderweb lines. But as she drew closer, Elathien noted that the fragments weren't simply cracked but had been wholly splintered and reshaped, held in perfect stasis by the force field that still bound them.

It had the look of a painting, a frozen moment of time. She saw the red-black stain held within the glass, spreading down along the wall and across the white tile of the floor. She saw the silver badge of the refuge, along with a sheathed dagger and what looked like a set of faith-caster's charms all soaking at the center of that pool of blood. Laicos was crouched before it all, just staring.

"Two accidental deaths by falling within three days," Elathien called out loudly. "More happenstance, I suppose. So what kind of supposition shall we make to go with it?"

Laicos leveled her a look that normally would have forced Elathien to suppress a smile. She was too tired this morning to take advantage of it, however.

"Mistress Elathien," the investigator said with forced formality. "Master Cirhela has once again expressed a desire for you to lend your expertise to this investigation."

"And good morning to you, too. Where is Cirhela?"

"Sitting for questioning." Off Elathien's look, he added, "Respectful questioning, I assure you."

"Of course."

"And though I'm sure it will be obvious even to you," Laicos said grimly, "this wasn't death by falling, any more than was the death of the magister. Our unfortunate sentry died when he went through the window of arcane force and the glass beyond it."

As they had approached the refuge, at Elathien's request, her Guard escort had led her past the even bloodier scene below the window. What was left of the body had been covered by layers of white cloth, stained through like a well-used butcher's smock. She hadn't asked to see beneath them, though she guessed by Laicos's grim expression that he had been obliged to.

"That takes a certain amount of perseverance." Elathien stepped close enough to trace a finger along the shimmering arcane field.

"Meaning it should be clear that he was forced," the investigator said with faintly disguised impatience. "I feel so fortunate that I have your insight to guide me in these matters."

"Laicos, you couldn't be bothered to even pretend an interest in the death of Magister Sirnos. Forgive my surprise at your sudden interest in treating this as an actual investigation." She caught the reactions of the two guards closest to her, an Ilvani giving her a dark look, a broad Essaruk flashing the grin that she knew hid even more disdain. She didn't care.

"One death unexplained casts its own shadow," the investigator said evenly, "and shows only the motive and intent of fate. Two deaths unexplained create patterns of darkness, in which the motive and intent of mortal desire might be seen. Bellas, in his work *On the Nature of Mortal Murder*. I'll do my best to find you a copy."

Elathien smiled this time. "No sign of struggle," she said as she knelt to survey the floor before the shattered window. The tiles were well worn, but showed no sign of recent scuff marks.

"None." Laicos gestured to the dagger. "If that blade was the sentry's, he was armed against refuge policy but left it in the sheath."

"Compulsion or enchantment," Elathien said, thoughtful. "Expecting trouble but unable to even respond to it. Did the sentry know Nerani or Irandis?"

She felt Laicos reject the question in the tone of his response. "The sentries cover the entire refuge, day and night. It's easy to assume that he interacted with one or both, but no records will ever show it."

"There's a connection between Sirnos and Irandis that Sirnos kept hidden…"

"Which will no doubt be taken into consideration. However, that's not the focus of the investigation at this stage…"

"Which undoubtedly involves searching for connections between this dead sentry and Sirnos. To deduce what common cause their accidental deaths might have had."

"The official status of the investigation is death by unknown means of arcana," Laicos said testily, "as it was originally. And seeking connections between two victims is standard procedure, is it not? The evidence at hand, the manner in which the sentry was destroyed, points to the undead, Master Cirhela's gallant defense of the senses of her healers notwithstanding."

"The undead kill with their own power, draining the force of life to leave a husk behind. Neither of these deaths show the signs. Your guess is that Sirnos was killed with his own magic turned against him, but unless this sentry was a secret sorcerer, that didn't happen last night. As such, you'd be wiser to look for an outside source of magic in both deaths."

"Thank you for your opinions," Laicos said evenly.

Elathien felt a retort die on her tongue. "Has the new victim been identified?" she said instead.

"The state of the body makes it a process of elimination," Laicos replied. "The sentry who should have been on patrol at the time of the death hasn't been seen since. Tajamynar, his name was. An Ilvani of the Yewnwood. He'd worked at the refuge nearly six years."

Elathien was at the shattered window again, but she glanced to Laicos in surprise at the name. "That's the sentry who found Magister Sirnos's body. I questioned him yesterday." From the investigator's expression, she guessed that he hadn't yet known either bit of information.

"You have a record of your questioning?"

"With Cirhela. Ask her for it. Politely if you can manage."

"Perhaps you can summarize," Laicos said darkly.

In her mind's eye, Elathien cast back to her conversation with the sentry. "Nothing special. No information beyond what was in the initial Guard patrol's report. He was nervous when he spoke, but no more so than any of the other sentries. Sirnos's murder on their watch has put them all on edge. One of their own dying will push things to the breaking point."

"Six sentries have already resigned, but the City Watch will send in support if need be. Sentries and healers alike, they're all talking about the Curse of Blackheath now."

"A most convenient response for an investigator. Because it means you can keep telling yourself there's nothing here to investigate."

As Elathien spoke, she wrapped her hand in her cloak, binding flesh with cloth as she had watched Nerani do. As she herself had done more than once, more than a year ago. She didn't look at Laicos as she carefully pushed into the force shield with her covered hand.

"The worst curses, the darkest magic in all the Elder Kingdoms is brought through these doors," Laicos said coldly. "Yet you'll maintain that has nothing to with the destruction seen here?"

"On the contrary. I believe it has everything to do with what happened here." As she pressed her fingers into it, Elathien felt the force field as a faint numbness, holding just at the threshold below real pain. The expanse of shattered glass held in stasis by that force began to ripple like waves on still water, rings of bright and shadow spreading from the center as they scattered the faint light of morning outside.

"If that was the case, Master Cirhela shouldn't have contacted the Yewnyr Guard. This would be a matter for the Authority Arcane."

"And you're smart enough to understand why Cirhela needs this to not become a matter for the Authority Arcane. Their first step would be to turn the entire population of convalescents out onto the streets so they could conduct their investigations without disturbance. The question of who's died here and why means nothing to them, as long as there's power to be gained."

"This is curse magic, clear as day, but you act as though this was a routine death investigation."

"Magic is a tool," Elathien said. "Magic is a weapon, and just as with any other weapon, you look for the hand behind it."

"You suppose murder?" Laicos scoffed. "The sentry, possibly. But a magister of Sirnos's power bettered by another spellcaster?"

"No." The razor-sharp fragments of glass were moving, Elathien saw, so very subtly. The field of force that held them in place was flowing in between the shards, so that they were pushed away from each other. Shivering restlessly as drops of blood flowed and congealed within their cracks. "But nothing happens without a reason. When a blade kills, look for the hand that wielded it. When a curse kills, look for the hand that unleashed it, whether intentionally or otherwise."

The windows of Blackheath were old magic, of the Empire dead and gone nearly fifty years before. For more than a thousand years, the Imperial mages alone had known the secrets of shaping dweomer to permanent forms. Though few could match that knowledge these days, Sirnos had been one of those, at least to judge by the power imbued into and channeled by the red-black crystal. Elathien found herself wondering idly whether there was anyone at the institute now with spellcraft enough to fix this window with Sirnos gone.

"I assume you also questioned the girl in your efforts yesterday?" Laicos asked.

"I met with her," Elathien said. She let the force field push her hand out, the pain spiking for a moment before it quelled. "Her fear and fragility don't allow for questioning."

"In your opinion."

"Leave her alone, Laicos." Elathien stepped close to the investigator, seeing a faint smirk twist through his expression.

"A strange reaction," Laicos said, "considering that you were the one accusing me of not taking her so-called prophetic vision seriously."

"My point was to wonder whether Nerani was a sensitive. Someone whose state of mind let her pick up on a faint connection to whatever curse was responsible for Magister Sirnos's death."

"And I applaud your insight. The girl will be questioned…"

"And your questions will force her deeper inside herself, keeping us from learning anything. You're a bigger fool than anyone who wears that uniform is allowed to be, Laicos."

"Better a fool than a renegade and traitor to the badge."

Elathien felt a caustic anger churn through the silence that suddenly filled her. So he had asked after her name from someone in the records hall of the Yewnyr Guard. No matter, she thought. That part of her life was hardly a secret anymore.

"I know you have a tight schedule of time-wasting to maintain," she said. An unintended bitterness threaded her voice, Laicos reacting to it with a thin smile. "I won't keep you."

But even as she turned and paced away from him, Elathien's line of thought was stopped suddenly by the appearance of a familiar face farther along the corridor. Lady Dacani was there, but Elathien hadn't noticed her where she stood well back in the shadows. Far from the action of the investigation, even as she watched it darkly from afar.

That was odd, Elathien thought as she stepped to a window alcove, staying out of sight as she watched. Dacani was Master Administrator of Blackheath. Rumors of a deadly curse and sentries defecting would both be her responsibility. She should have been front and center in the investigation, alternately leading it or engaged in a hand-to-hand struggle for authority with Laicos's team.

In Dacani's gaze, Elathien saw the same cold anger she had seen in the magister's office two days before. But beneath it, barely visible through the officious mask, was something else. Fear.

At her side, Diranta set up a low growl, just loud enough for her to hear.

Elathien scanned the corridor around and behind her, cautious suddenly. Laicos was busy talking to a group of Blackheath sentries, their looks dark as he undoubtedly sought and found ways to question their professionalism. Lady Dacani was moving, heading down the corridor and away from her, but it was the doorway adjacent to where the administrator had been standing that the dog was focused on, nostrils flaring.

Elathien gave him the signal to lead. Diranta moved, making a beeline for the closed door at a quick walk. She followed carefully, letting one hand slip to her back and the hilts of her knives beneath her cloak. She was on edge suddenly, the previous night's uneasy sleep not helping her already distracted senses.

Diranta was nose down to the ground, tracking by scent. But for the life of her, Elathien had no idea who he could possibly be following. Not having been in Blackheath until this morning, the only person whose scent the dog knew here was Cirhela. However, he had no reason to show the enmity toward the healer that he was showing now, his tail down as he hunted.

Or was it some sense other than scent that drew him on?

Ahead, Elathien thought she saw a figure slip through a shadowed archway. They were away from the wards, near to one of the towers, she guessed, but her sense of direction had been lost to the turns in the course the dog followed. The figure was moving quickly, a blur of grey, but whether the gown of a convalescent or the tunic of a worker, Elathien couldn't tell. She gave Diranta the signal to close.

With a lunge, the dog took off at a run, feet padding loudly across the stone floors as she sprinted to follow. He tore through the archway a half-dozen steps ahead of her, but Elathien was brought up short by a startled voice.

"Diranta!"

She skidded to a stop as she saw Cirhela pressed back against the wall. Diranta was circling around her, whining as he tried in vain to pick up the scent he'd been following. The floors of the corridor were damp with a trace of wash water, the scent of lye on the air.

"Sorry," Elathien said. She signaled Diranta to stand down, though she knew that Cirhela was more surprised than afraid. "Did you see someone come through here? A convalescent or sentry?"

"No one passed by me. I only heard you running. What's going on?"

Elathien crouched to scan the floor, Diranta still whining where he sat at her side. She gave him the signal to track again, but he simply circled across the corridor, confused. It made no sense, she thought. Even if the lye was interfering with Diranta's ability to catch a scent, she should have seen footprints passing along the faint sheen of the flagstones. However, the floor was clear except for Cirhela's tracks tracing back along the corridor.

Elathien whispered the cantrip of detection, feeling the strength of her spellpower spreading out from her, seeking for the telltale signs of dweomer in the corridor. She was quick enough that only the weakest magic would have had time to fade, but even still, she felt nothing except the aura of the keys at Cirhela's belt. The rest of the corridor was clear.

"Elathien? What's going on?" the healer asked again.

"It's said that animals can sense the power of certain undead," Elathien said thoughtfully.

"Some undead, yes. Spectral presences. The darkest shades." Cirhela glanced down to where she stroked Diranta's head. "You think that's what he was chasing?"

"I don't know what he was chasing. I just know it was something he recognized, as if by instinct."

"The wards against undead are as strong in Blackheath as they are anywhere in the Elder Kingdoms. For such a presence to linger here without any of the healers becoming aware of it, without me being aware of it, is impossible."

Cirhela's words carried the quiet confidence Elathien had always heard in her. She understood that anyone who didn't know the healer as well as she did would have seen her as the picture of composure at first glance. But as she appraised the healer's expression, she couldn't help but note the darkness there.

"I'm sorry about what's happened," Elathien said, her tone more awkward than she liked. "The magister's death and the sentry's, I mean. I know what you must be going through."

"People are scared," Cirhela said. But her own face showed none of that fear, Elathien saw. Only the same control, the same authority she had seen that first morning after Magister Sirnos died, when the healer arrived on her doorstep. "I need to fix it."

And as Cirhela said the words, Elathien understood suddenly the nature of the healer's careful thought. Driven to fix what she saw broken in others as always, she was focused on their fear. But in that focus, she had become too scared on behalf of those others to face her own fear.

In the intense year when they met, over the long months of her healing, then what had come after, Elathien had learned that more than anything else, Cirhela needed to believe in the good. Not in the sense of any simple morality of faith, for which Cirhela had as little patience as Elathien did. The sense that even within the more complex morality of the real world, good would triumph over darkness in the end.

"Laicos said the Guard had spoken to you," Elathien said absently. Not sure what else she could say.

"Yes. There'll be more questions for everyone, I'm sure."

"Including Nerani," Elathien said. "Which means we need to talk to her first."

— TEN —

THE GIRL'S BEDCHAMBER was far too uncomfortably familiar to Elathien where she stood at the narrow window. The simple cell resembled all the other chambers of the convalescents' wards, its walls of well-patched plaster showing the faint ripples of timeless layers of whitewash.

Nerani sat at the edge of the plain pallet, her head hung low, hair shrouding her eyes. Cirhela was in the room's only other piece of furniture, a straight-backed chair that she had pulled out from the corner opposite the open door. Both she and Elathien had greeted Nerani as they entered, but had gotten no response. Both of them were simply waiting now. As they did, however, Elathien could see the girl watching Diranta from the corner of her eye, so she motioned for him to sit at the foot of the bed.

"You can call him to you," she said carefully, as much to break the silence as anything. "His name is Diranta." The dog's tail struck the floor twice in recognition.

It was warm on the ward, so Elathien had taken off her leather tunic in favor of the plain white shift beneath it. The tattoos of her shoulders were visible but she didn't care. When the forces of the Guard had dragged her from her bed before dawn, her only priority had been to dress for a day of not knowing where she'd be or what she might be doing. The decision to bring the dog with her had been made on the same grounds, but she was glad of his presence now.

Too many things were going on around her, too many things she couldn't see, as with the scent Diranta had picked up and pursued in the corridor. Spectral presences, she thought. Dark shades. Elathien still had no idea what she was dealing with, but with the sentry's death, things had changed. As much as anything else, she wanted to be able to eliminate the things she wasn't dealing with.

Cautiously, she flicked her fingers for Diranta, motioning him to nuzzle Nerani where she sat. He did so carefully, Nerani's hands finding his head easily, stroking him. Elathien felt the girl's mood soften.

"A sentry was killed last night," she said carefully. She acknowledged Cirhela's look of caution, but the girl said nothing in response. She was focused on Diranta where he arched his head up, letting her fingers trace across his shoulders and long neck. "He fell and died, the same as the magister who died two nights past. The same as Irandis."

It was only a slight bending of the truth, but Elathien thought it necessary. Not wanting to overwhelm the girl with the full scope of what was happening. Or perhaps waiting to see if she already knew those details.

"Nerani." Cirhela's voice was even, probing carefully at the girl's silence. "Elathien and I think that what's happening at Blackheath might have something to do with you. Perhaps in ways you don't even…"

"My mother… lived in refuge," the girl whispered. "At the great house of Maera the Huntress. In Anduras." She leaned into Diranta, the dog accepting her embrace in a way that Elathien recognized. It was a way he had of sensing vulnerability, of showing that his instincts recognized no threat in the girl. "My father died. In the work gangs, six years after I was born…"

The words came from her in fits and starts, Nerani shivering suddenly in a way that silenced Cirhela. A tremor twisted through her like the sudden confession was laced with a pain that shot her to her feet, sent her stumbling back along the wall. Diranta backed away, cautious. Nerani's eyes were wide, looking up to meet Elathien's gaze.

"I didn't know that before," the girl said shakily. "I've forgotten so many things."

"Nerani…"

"Irandis lived in Thaelind Heights. Since her eighth summer. She was lost…" Nerani clutched at the window as if she might fall, Cirhela and Elathien moving for her at the same time. They stood close at either side, Cirhela with her arm around Nerani's waist. Elathien held back, trying to assess the level of consciousness in the girl's eyes and not liking what she was seeing.

"By the time of her twelfth summer, she'd been arrested by the watch for the fourth time. Sent to the work gangs herself, no clemency."

"We know what kind of life Irandis had," Cirhela said. "We know what it did to her…"

"You know nothing!"

Nerani's unexpected shout carried through her open door and across the ward, splintering distant voices to doubtful silence. She was breathing hard, her hands shaking. Elathien saw the girl's fingers twisting in pain, the muscles of her thin arms locked tight. At a glance, she appeared terrified, but the spastic reaction carried a telltale slowness. An uncertainty. This was more than fear, more than memory.

"Enchantment," Elathien mouthed to Cirhela, who acknowledged with a dark look. Even as the healer whispered the incantation of detection, Elathien whispered to Nerani's ear.

"Then tell us, Nerani. Make us understand."

The girl's breathing rasped in her chest, fighting to squeeze through the sob that choked her. "I don't want to talk..."

"But you do, Nerani." Elathien shifted to try to make eye contact. "You told me Irandis was murdered. You said you knew how it happened. You want to speak of these things. Don't let them stay inside where all they can do is hurt you."

She caught Cirhela's eye where the healer read the magic that all of Elathien's instincts told her was controlling the girl now. But to her surprise, Cirhela shook her head. No spell of compulsion was in Nerani. No enchantment or channeling.

"But you don't believe it," Nerani hissed. "You don't listen to me, so that what they say becomes the truth of silence. Because whatever I say to you, whatever you pretend it means, when I'm done talking, you'll be outside these walls. And I'll be gone."

Nerani lurched as a tremor twisted through her. Both arms were up, hands bunched to fists as she struck at the window, its shimmering screen of force flaring white as the pain pushed her stumbling back. If Cirhela hadn't been holding her, she would have fallen. As it was, it took both the healer and Elathien to lower the girl back to the pallet. She was shivering, eyes wide.

"Nerani, who are 'they'? *What they say becomes the truth,* you said. Whose truth?"

Cirhela made as if to interrupt, but Elathien silenced her with a hand clasped to hers. She squeezed it tight to feel it shaking, knowing that the healer wanted the girl to stop. But Elathien needed Nerani to speak, because she knew the pain in the girl's voice from all the times she'd felt that pain herself. The truth tearing you apart inside, needing to come out.

"The ones who killed her," the girl whispered. "Because they were afraid of her. Because they knew that no one would care enough to miss her when she was gone."

Head down on Cirhela's shoulder, Nerani was overcome with sobbing. But even as Elathien put a hand to the girl's back, feeling the tremor thread through it, she saw that no tears traced her face. Nerani's eyes were dry, even as all the emotion of a forgotten lifetime spilled from her.

When the girl quieted, Elathien spoke again.

"Nerani, I don't know that Irandis was murdered. But I do know that she was afraid. I know that people hurt her, and every part of me would like to see those people pay for what they did. But judgement isn't always our right, even when it's deserved."

Nerani was silent for a long moment before she spoke. "You don't believe in justice?"

There was an edge to that last word in the girl's young voice, Elathien thought. Like it was a thing she might never have said before, testing its unfamiliar syllables. "I don't believe in vengeance."

And even as Elathien spoke the words, she felt Nerani's trembling body suddenly go still. Cirhela reacted instantly, but the girl's breathing was steady, her back straight against the wall. Her eyes were wide, staring darkly at nothing. It was the appearance of having a charm broken, Elathien noted. The charm that Cirhela's magic had said wasn't there.

"I don't want to talk," Nerani said.

"Nerani..." Elathien began, but Cirhela cut her off.

"No." She heard an edge of warning in the voice. Something in the sudden change of Nerani's mood that the healer recognized, Elathien guessed. She only nodded as she stood and stepped away.

In the ward sitting room, light at the narrow windows faded and flared as cloud crossed the sun-streaked sky. Elathien lingered in the doorway as Cirhela laid Nerani down, her arm around the girl's waist as she whispered to her ear. The words were unheard, but Elathien could feel them just the same. She remembered the blank look she saw on the girl's face. She remembered the healer's arm around her own shoulder, the touch and the words trying to take that emptiness away.

She signaled to Diranta, who crossed to her side. He watched the girl intently, but his tail was up, she noted. The wellspring of pain and emotion in Nerani's room was something he could feel, but still, it didn't faze him. None of the dark energy was in him that he had shown when tracking the mysterious trail of that morning.

Neither Cirhela nor Nerani looked up to see Elathien and the dog slip away.

It was later when Cirhela found her again, and in a place where Elathien wouldn't have expected her to look.

From Nerani's room, she had drifted down to the kitchens, her dark mood not helped by the fact that her abrupt morning departure from her flat meant she hadn't yet eaten. From the days she spent in Blackheath before, Elathien knew that the meat of the kitchens was of good quality and recent vintage, even if lacking in spice. She knew also how to quietly pay the cooks to turn a blind eye as she helped herself at the larder, stuffing cold mutton and pickle into a heel of bread, then slipping it to her pocket in a clean headscarf.

With Diranta close at her heels, she wandered up to the rooftop garden, hoping that the chill of the season would offer some privacy. She was thus surprised to see figures beyond the frost-streaked glass of windows and doors as she stepped through.

A dozen figures stood in a circle beneath the bare trees, branches twisting in the chill wind to scrape the bright blue sky. Elathien had to step closer to hear their voices, though. She recognized the low chant of an Ilvani memorial service, not needing to guess who it was for. Sentries were well represented among the mourners for the dead Tajamynar, set among the ranks of healers and orderlies that crowded around a young priest. Elathien didn't recognize the names of the gods they were praying to, but she had never been much good at keeping such things straight.

She didn't stay long enough to listen in, feeling a sense of having intruded in a private moment even despite her dismissal of the ritual's intent. Even from childhood, Elathien had never felt any great attraction to faith. When all was said and done, finding faith in herself seemed enough of a challenge sometimes.

From the garden, she made her way into the Masters' Tower. Twice, she slipped into alcoves to avoid footsteps passing along side corridors on the way to her ultimate destination. That was Lady Dacani's office, its black door responding in silence to Elathien's knock, then yielding only with difficulty to her lockpicks. She summoned up the cantrip of detection at once as she and Diranta slipped inside.

Even with no response to her knock, she half-expected to see Lady Dacani looking up from her desk in outrage as she closed the door behind her. The office was unoccupied, though, Elathien making a careful sweep for any magic of warding or alarm. She found nothing, as she expected, knowing that such spellcraft wasn't the administrator's style. Whatever secrets she was hiding, Dacani would have concealed them by less subtle means.

Elathien sat to eat, braiding her hair as she did. A glassed mirror on Lady Dacani's bookshelf reminded her how haggard she looked in the aftermath of two nights of little sleep. The office around her was an opulent space of leather and old wood. Black-spined books lined tall shelves, blinds of cloth drawn across the refuge's familiarly narrow windows. Statuary and art were set sparsely around the room, all of it in a contemporary style whose lack of any adherence to natural form made Elathien vaguely uneasy.

What Elathien had seen of Dacani that morning suggested the administrator was anxious to avoid the Yewnyr Guard's investigation, even as a sense of obligation to the refuge would have forced her to hole up somewhere accessible to that investigation if it came looking for her. But if Dacani was hiding somewhere other than her office, it suggested that her reasons for not being in the thick of things carried a secrecy that Elathien didn't like.

No matter for now, though. She could find enough things to keep herself occupied until Lady Dacani returned.

Elathien relied on instinct and feel as she set about on a most thorough search of the office. Her repertoire of spells included a small number that might have aided her, but the spellpower was flagging in her and she was reluctant to fully exhaust it. The brief amount of sleep she had managed before being woken that morning had replenished only a fraction of the magic she expended the previous day. That day's spellpower had been flagging already, her night at Cirhela's giving her little opportunity to sleep.

The relative tedium of her search through shelves and files, drawers and scrolls, let her replenish an additional minimal amount of arcane strength. However, the full rest she should have taken would have required a focus and a calm that all her instincts said was beyond her right now.

That lack of focus meant that she wasn't fully aware of how much time had passed when she heard the door open. She hadn't even heard the key at the lock, looking up in surprise to see Cirhela watching her.

The healer's eyes took in the room at a glance where Elathien had carefully taken it apart. Books were pulled from shelves and stacked across the desk and floor. The desk was open, the contents of its unlocked drawers spread out on chairs. When Cirhela's eyes flicked back to hers, Elathien registered that the healer didn't seem surprised to see her.

"You've been busy," Cirhela said.

"How did you know I was here?" Elathien replied by way of not answering.

"Maintaining knowledge of someone you know isn't difficult with the right magic at hand."

Elathien was surprised at that, and tired enough that she knew Cirhela could tell. "Needing that kind of control seems unlike you. Or have things changed that much since the last time we saw each other?"

"Blackheath holds a dozen spellcasters who answer to me as a member of the Council of Masters. With them to do my bidding, I wouldn't need to worry about hurting your feelings."

"Having the authority and the power to impose your will on someone is one thing," Elathien said. "But I'd be surprised if you ever actually did it." She moved back to the desk, a stack of notes set down beside her as she sat.

Cirhela sighed as she shook her head. "I've been looking for you the old-fashioned way," she said. "But as long as you don't tell people where you're going, you might get that surprise one day."

Elathien ignored the weight of the comment as the healer crossed to the windows. Streaks of sunset were darkening the sky, causing Elathien to blink in surprise. Even as early as the winter sunset fell, she hadn't noticed the day fading so quickly away.

"You've been busy," Cirhela said again.

"I'm just waiting for inspiration."

"As always."

Elathien sifted two of the stacks of paper on the desk, thoughtfully pulling new notes to the top of each. "How is Nerani? Since this morning, I mean."

"Her mental and spiritual state has regressed. Her behavior is similar to what it was when she was first found. As quickly as she progressed since then, she's regressing now just as fast."

"But that would suggest that her condition is cyclical, wouldn't it? That she'll come back the other way?"

"I don't know. I hope so."

The arrangement of documents in front of Elathien would have made no sense to anyone who looked. It made no sense to her, in fact. Not as yet, anyway. But as she'd rifled through Lady Dacani's files and let the day pass by without her knowing, she had been working within the feeling that something was there, still unseen.

"Do you know what it is you're looking for?" Cirhela asked, as though she could read Elathien's train of thought.

"Lady Dacani, mostly. And wondering why she hasn't burst in here yet to lay down her extremely dire threats. Have you seen her today?"

"No," Cirhela said. "I would have assumed she'd be with Laicos and his people."

"She was keeping clear of Laicos this morning. And even assuming he caught up to her at some point, I doubt he'd keep her the entire day." Elathien sat back and stretched, feeling something twinge as she twisted her shoulders. She'd been sitting too long.

"The masters are meeting at sunset," Cirhela said evenly. "She might be working with them individually before then. Trying to gather enough support that she can be the one to suggest that the refuge be closed."

"That's a bit premature, isn't it?"

"Two deaths over two nights. The situations we've had here before, the incidents, the accidents. There's been nothing like this in long years."

"Blackheath is a place where the darkest curses in five lands are mastered and unwrought. As horrifying as these deaths are, it's hard to believe that they're so far beyond the scope of what the healers and staff have faced before."

"Two people have been not only slain but destroyed. It's not just the power. It's the evil that seems to twist through that power. A sense of malevolence. No explanations."

"As long as there's no explanation, that should make finding an explanation the masters' only priority." Elathien stepped to the closest wall sconce to dim the evenlamp in its shroud.

"I should have you speak to them for me, then."

Elathien felt an unaccustomed anger in the healer's voice, and though she knew it wasn't meant for her, it made it more awkward when she said, "I need to go."

"I didn't mean to drive you away…"

"You didn't," Elathien said, too quickly. "I need to go to Anduras Hamlets. The things Nerani said this morning, her mother, her father. It bears investigating."

"Then you think there is an explanation?" Cirhela looked back from the window, dark hair framing her face.

"There are always explanations." Elathien stood and stepped to the window, facing Cirhela where she leaned against the sill. She felt the chill of the approaching night through heavy glass, no field of force here to block it. "Power manifests," she said. "Magic, politics, wealth, hatred. It's all the same. Things are set in motion, they collide with other things. It's an easy supposition that the power that killed here originated with

Sirnos. Some curse or spell unleashed that killed him by accident, and whose residual energy is what killed the sentry. But that focuses the investigation only on what can be sensed, on what can be seen. A true investigator can seek beyond that, to what can only be felt."

"But the notion that Sirnos unleashed a curse makes perfect sense. The secrets of his that you've discovered, the things he's been involved in. It should be easy to believe."

"It's not that I don't believe it," Elathien said. "But that side of the story is irrelevant to the kind of understanding I want. A curse is a weapon. All magic is a weapon, the same as any blade, any bow in a hand that knows how to use it. I'm interested in whose hand is ultimately holding the weapon."

"Then you see intent in what's happened here?"

"Quite the opposite. Intent speaks to goal and focus, but what's happened here has no focus. The decision to kill can be methodical. It can be made rationally enough. But the decision to inflict the kind of suffering that's been seen here, to tear someone limb from limb with magic, isn't made by the mind. You talked about evil, but this is beyond evil. It's a decision made in the heart, in a moment of madness."

Cirhela had turned to the window again. Elathien watched her carefully, assessing a degree of calm in the healer that she knew marked Cirhela's greatest strength and greatest weakness.

"The arcane is the boundary between the unliving world and the living mind," Elathien said evenly. "Where the mind is broken, the power can be tapped that much more easily. A trauma manifests itself as an imprint on the mind. That imprint reflects through the potential for magic to create an effect in the physical world. The dark energy of this place, the potential for destruction in whatever illegal magic Magister Sirnos was engaged in creates a well of potential."

Like she had seen earlier, there was no fear in Cirhela now. Nothing that would break her strength of heart and the will that told her anything was possible. But that lack of fear was a liability in situations like this one. Situations worthy of fear.

"Magic is ultimately uncontrollable," Elathien said, "so it's easy to assume it has no causality. Laicos has no chance of solving this mystery because he doesn't believe it can be solved. He sees the magic underlying this mystery as chaos. He sees madness, driven by forces that can't be known, can't be shaped or directed."

"That concept of madness means nothing to me," Cirhela said. "You know that. There's no ill that can't be cured. No conscious hatred deep enough to take responsibility for what happened to Magister Sirnos, to that poor sentry."

"But what about an unconscious hatred?" As she continued around the room, Elathien replaced books on their shelves. "Nerani's belief that Irandis was murdered might be strong enough that it becomes its own kind of power. Not focused spellcraft, or even blood magic. Something else."

While Elathien restored the scene of her search, the healer was moving along the wall opposite, dimming the lamps there. "You don't think Nerani is the weapon." Not a question. The sudden fall of shadow spilled out from the already dark corners of the room, setting up a bright reflection in the healer's eyes.

"No," Elathien said. "But she could be the trigger. A catalyst, tapping into that latent energy." Cirhela's scent seemed stronger somehow in the shadows, she thought. Rose and lilac.

The healer stepped close to her, warm where she pressed in against her shoulder. Elathien made a mental note that it would be prudent to move, even as she knew she had no intention of doing so.

Elathien felt Diranta's low growl almost before she heard it.

The dog was pointed at the closed door in a low crouch, lips curled to show the gleam of his canines. Though the dense curls of his hackles were too thick to truly rise, Elathien saw the ridged muscles of his neck tensed.

"A spell of detection," she whispered. "Now."

Without hesitation, Cirhela clutched at the sigil of Blackheath at her shoulder that was the symbol and focus of her power, whispering an animyst incantation as her hand shaped the spell. Elathien followed suit with her own magic, feeling the sharp contrast between the intricate weave of the arcane force and the simpler patterns of the healer's life-magic. Both of them shifted around the desk, feeling the power of their very different spells unfurl through the solid barriers of door and wall as if they might be fog burning away at the touch of the dawn.

Elathien felt it. In the corridor beyond the door, the shape of dweomercraft waxed as a field of arcane potential that impressed itself on her mind like the touch of an unremembered dream. She focused it, tried to hold it as she pulled the door open. But even as she touched the handle, she felt that unseen magic suddenly wink out.

In her mind was a moment of emptiness that matched the emptiness of the corridor. The feel of a soap bubble popping, if such a thing could be rendered as touch. The hall was dimly lit to both sides, but that was enough to see no sign of anyone there.

Elathien had a long-knife in her hand as she pressed back to the wall. She couldn't remember drawing it. Diranta whined as he circled with his nose to the cold tile of the floor. He was growling again as he picked up a scent — the same as that he had keyed on earlier, Elathien guessed. Something or someone he knew and disliked.

"Did you sense anything?" she whispered to Cirhela as she motioned for the dog to hold.

"Nothing of undead energy. You?"

"Magic. Not long enough to get a sense of its power, but it's gone now. It's likely an item dweomer, no lingering aura left. Someone teleporting." Absently, she touched her cloak to feel the steel talisman she had found in Irandis's flat still there. She had yet to discern its power, but that was a thing she needed to rectify.

"Who? And why?"

"Let's find out."

With a snap of her fingers, Elathien released Diranta. Silent except for the low growl of satisfaction at taking up the chase, the dog tore along the corridor in the direction of the scent he had picked up. Behind him, Elathien and Cirhela followed at a run.

— ELEVEN —

THE GARDEN WAS EMPTY, the sky dark above the towers that marked the corners of the rooftop. In the shadows, Lady Dacani could see the offerings left from that morning's rites, the permission for which had been one of the day's many details that blurred in her mind now. She had approached the open space between the trees more than once as she paced the garden's gravel paths, but never too closely. Never bothering to hide her unease. The talk of the spirit and the soul, the ceremony of all that superstition. None of it meant anything to her.

Lingering small in the shadows, she kept the hood of her cloak up to shroud her face, watching always for signs of anyone approaching. She hadn't been waiting long, but she was already feeling anxious about being seen — and by one person in particular. Cirhela's investigator. Not the Yewnyr Guard sergeant, but the wild one. Elathien.

Lady Dacani had watched her that morning, sparring verbally with the sergeant investigator whose ineptitude Dacani was counting on to preclude any quick resolution to the institute's present strife. The chaos that Sirnos had brought down upon them needed to stay unsettled, for a while at least. Dacani had used that chaos to her advantage earlier that day, working her way one by one through the other members of the Council of Masters. Getting them behind her, convincing them privately that she was the best choice to chart a course through the uncertainty. Setting herself into a position of power, through which she would control the damage that the magister had wrought.

She was waiting for someone, and growing angrier the longer he delayed. She had passed him in the refuge that morning, when he had whispered the details of this meeting. *The garden at sunset.* Dacani felt the black gemstone in the inside pocket of her cloak, but she dared not use it. With Elathien having gone through Magister Sirnos's offices so thoroughly, it was beyond likely that the galling investigator was the reason the magister's gem, the third of the set, was gone. Lady Dacani didn't know if possessing one of the stones would allow Elathien to tap into the thoughts that passed between the other two, but she had no intention of finding out.

In her capacity as administrator of Blackheath and its operations, spellcasters of all stripes were answerable to Dacani. However, as one who had never felt the call of eldritch power, she distrusted that power more than she ever let any of her subordinates know. As such, she hadn't understood the full implications of Sirnos's plans even as she agreed to them. Now, pacing in the garden awaiting the one from whom Sirnos had taken his orders, it was far too late to dwell on that.

Privately, she had wept over Sirnos, though it had been years since the series of very private and ill-advised trysts between her and the magister. Lady Dacani had craved control of the power he represented, and his obvious interest made her bed seem an easy place to shape that power. In the end, however, Sirnos drove her away by virtue of coveting a dark control of his own.

When what was left of the sentry Tajamynar had been found in the deep night, Lady Dacani's only thoughts had been for herself. She wasn't afraid, though. Not exactly. The things she had seen, the power still at her disposal, allowed her to focus the certainty that would carry her through this affair. The control she set over the institute was exacting, and it would save her in the end.

Sirnos had been the one who had chosen the garden for their secret meetings. A place outside, he had called it. A place away from the arcanism and animys of the institute, and protected by the magic of druidas that permeated its stones. Lady Dacani felt that magic now in the subtle warmth of the night air, not as cold here between the trees as she knew it was on the street below.

Still, she couldn't stop shivering as she stared around her, catching the steady flare of light through the white-brushed touch of frost at the glass doors. She paced to warm herself, staring out to the glimmering dark of the city night, firelight and drifting smoke caught in the still air.

Behind her, Lady Dacani heard a faint rattling of glass.

The doors that she had just turned from were gleaming, their veneer of frost suddenly gone so that she could see her reflection, starlit and faint. That reflection was trembling as the glass trembled, just slightly. Subtly. Shimmering as if a passing wind had pulled at the panes, even as the air of the garden was still.

Dacani stumbled backward, one boot slipping on the frosted stones. As she fought to right herself, she felt a hand on her shoulder.

She tried to scream as she wheeled, but her voice was gone to a fear that she'd never known before. The girl's eyes were blank where she stood stock still in the center of the path. She wore the thin grey gown of a convalescent, no cloak against the cold, so that her hand was freezing to the touch as it shakingly stroked Lady Dacani's cheek.

One hand came up to strike the girl's arm away, even as the other lashed out hard across her face. The distant look in the young eyes showed her shock at being struck as she lurched back, bare feet slipping as she fell to the frost-bright ground. Then Dacani was running for the doors, the panes of those doors and the wide windows shaking now.

She was two steps away when the glass shattered. A storm wind erupted from nowhere to force Dacani back, sending her stumbling. It twisted around to scour her in a cloud of razor-sharp shards that turned her cloak to tatters, flensed her flesh to the bone with indescribable agony, pushed inside her to slice her lips and tongue to ribbons of ruined flesh as she tried to scream.

The last thing she saw as the shard storm blinded her was the girl, still on the ground where she had fallen. A fear was in the young eyes, mouth set in horror at what she saw. Her lip was bleeding where Dacani had struck her. She raised one hand, fist clenched as she wiped it absently across her mouth.

Then the girl's trembling fingers opened as if forced, and what had been Lady Dacani unfurled in a vortex of slivered glass, flesh and blood, shattered bone. The haze of starlight above the garden turned red-black for a moment, then the gale was gone and the wind had stilled to dead air once more. A swirling shape hung suspended in the air, then collapsed in a steaming heap to the ground. Only the vaguest humanoid form was suggested in its gruesome pattern. A figure with arms outreached, beseeching for escape from an unimaginable pain.

At the center of the ruin, enough of Lady Dacani's face remained to be recognizable, staring upward with sightless eyes, mouth open in an unfinished scream.

The spot stood empty where the girl, weeping at the sight before her, had turned her head away at the last.

By the time they got there, it was too late.

The scent that Diranta followed had circled back toward the garden, so that Elathien caught an unsettling sense of their destination long before they came to it. And not just the destination, she realized as she followed the dog at a run along shadowed corridors. Whoever's trail Diranta was following, that unknown figure had followed Elathien's exact course from the garden that morning. The same route that would have resulted either from her having been watched, or from the tracking magic she had foolishly accused Cirhela of using.

In the near distance, they heard the scream of the healer who was the first one to see what was left of Lady Dacani.

The initial moments of their arrival were a blur. Elathien noted the glass of the doors and windows shattered, but Cirhela was first to realize what it was they saw in the red-black shadows ahead. She quickly stumbled back to be sick in response. Elathien held onto the back of Diranta's neck for a moment to give her strength. Then she stepped through what was left of the doors.

She glanced to Lady Dacani's face only long enough to recognize it. With the incantation of detection, she felt the lingering traces of the magic that had caused the destruction. It twisted now through what the body had become, the field of bloodstained shards, the air itself. Even given the brief time that had passed, the level of fading dweomer carried a rare potency and a complex weave of arcane and animys power.

As she felt it fading, Elathien focused, reading the telltale secrets of that weave. Enchantment, the magic of the mind. Necromancy, darkness and death. The same threads of dweomer she had sensed in the red-black crystal found in Magister Sirnos's office, but so much more powerful than even the magic the crystal held.

Though the dweomer faded, a stronger point of magic remained behind, embedded in the field of gore and bone fragments. Elathien had to force her breathing to slow, approaching close enough to prod the spot with a broken length of alder branch. A cracked black gemstone emerged from the gore, radiating the dweomer of sending. Elathien left it there as she turned away.

From behind her came shouting voices that she realized were directed at her. Three Blackheath sentries were angrily calling her back as they warned away straggling healers and staff approaching along the adjacent corridors, trying to take control.

She ignored them except to shout back. "Find the sergeant investigator of the Guard. Laicos." She saw a shaking Cirhela being led away by a guard already on the scene, wrapping her shaking shoulders in his black and red cloak. On the opposite side of the rooftop, Diranta was circling, trying to catch a scent in a way that told Elathien there was nothing there.

She felt a faint fear twist through her as she checked the pouch at her belt. The crystal was still there, wrapped tightly in its lead sheath. She exposed one corner and felt its magic spike against the detection still threading her mind, as potent as it had been before. Nothing suggested that the crystal could have had anything to do with this event, but the resonant echo of those magical patterns was unmistakable. Too similar for it to be mere chance.

"You again. At the center of everything, it seems." As he stepped through into the chill air of the garden, Laicos was breathing hard, presumably having sprinted up from whatever lower level he had been on. "What are you doing here?"

"Your job," Elathien replied, weary. "You're looking for someone with teleportation magic. Likely a spellcaster from the evidence of what he's done here, but he uses the magic of an item to move. I've felt him twice so far."

"I'll thank you to answer my questions when they're put to you." Laicos's tone was dark as he slowly circled what was left of the body, taking in the scene with a shaky gaze. "Explain your presence here, now."

To Elathien's eye, the young sergeant was having trouble controlling the nausea twisting through him as he swallowed hard, fighting to slow his breathing. She saw his hand make the moonsign, out of sight of the four guards under his command where they held back.

"Following the killer. Master Cirhela and I were in Lady Dacani's offices. He was outside the door before he vanished. He was here beforehand. He must have come back to attack Lady Dacani."

Even as she said it, though, Elathien realized she was wrong.

Around them, two of the Guard were setting up magical evenlamps, their white light turning the dark stain that was Lady Dacani to a slickly glistening red. But before the leading edge of that stain, the administrator's bootprints in the frost of the gravel pathway showed a steady pacing track, back and forth through the shadows.

"Where is Lady Cirhela now?"

Elathien felt Laicos's voice slipping away. She felt the scene around her slow down, felt herself slip inside it to let the images and impressions fall into place. By the look of those tracks, Lady Dacani had been waiting here for far longer that it would have taken the unknown assailant to walk from the garden to the administrator's offices.

"The assailant and the teleporter who made the walk from here weren't the same person," she said thoughtfully.

"I asked the whereabouts of Lady Cirhela." In Laicos's voice, Elathien heard an edge of dark exasperation, but the way he ignored her line of thought bothered her more.

"She went with one of your people. She looked shaken up."

"Was she witness to this event?"

"Neither of us was. We saw what you see."

And even as she looked again to the grisly scene, Elathien understood something. The animosity she had felt toward Lady Dacani. The anger in Magister Sirnos's office. She knew suddenly where it came from.

The long-ago meetings from which she remembered Dacani's face had been the final and most challenging part of her time at Blackheath. Elathien had only been vaguely aware at the time how hard Cirhela was fighting for her, setting up the legal challenges that opened up the opportunity for Elathien to win her freedom from her family's control of her.

"Talk to the refuge's sentry sergeants," she said to Laicos, distracted. "Ask to see the duty logs from a month past. They'll tell you that the sentry who was murdered last night was the one who left the Laboratory Tower unlocked the night Irandis died."

Two days before, Dacani had recognized her in Sirnos's office. The administrator had remembered her name, had seemingly recalled the details of the case that had brought Elathien to Blackheath. One convalescent among hundreds, but Dacani remembered her. And so Elathien had sensed but not been able to focus on the most obvious explanation for that familiarity.

She wondered now whether Dacani had been working for her family then. Quietly fighting to keep Elathien where she was, hidden away in Blackheath to avoid embarrassment. Her family's status and station causing them to fear the public backlash that Elathien had delivered to them tenfold once she eventually secured her release.

Laicos didn't bother to hide his derision as he laughed. "Again, the dead sister. Three victims of the curse in front of you, yet you waste your time…"

"Laicos, it makes no difference to me how badly you undermine your place in the Guard by your stupidity and your stubbornness, but as long as you're working this investigation, you'll have an easier time seeing what's in front of you the faster you pull your head from your ass."

Elathien's voice was pitched just loud enough for the closest members of the Guard to hear, and Laicos knew it.

"I will not be lectured by the likes of you…"

"Yes, you will, and you'll thank me when I'm done. The sentry Tajamynar was the one who left the doors unlocked. Magister Sirnos undertook counseling with Irandis that produced the same veiled threats seen in the note that her sister Nerani wrote again a week after Irandis was dead. Lady Dacani was the administrator responsible for dealing with the consequences of that death. If Irandis was murdered, those three would have to be part of it. If you want to know more, you'll come with me now. I might even let you pretend you're the one leading me."

She turned on her heel, calling Diranta to her with a snap of her fingers. She didn't have to look back to hear Laicos following, stepping quickly to get abreast of her as they went.

— TWELVE —

ELATHIEN LEFT DIRANTA on guard outside the door to Lady Dacani's offices, not taking any chance that the teleporter would surprise her a third time. Inside, the last of the files were spread on the desk where she had left them.

A moment's worry made her wonder whether the mystery figure had doubled back while she and Cirhela followed the trail to the garden. She measured the placement and position of the papers against her memory, noting no sign of anything having been disturbed from before. But was that because whoever had followed her to the office had no interest in what might be found in Lady Dacani's files, meaning that Elathien alone was the target of the unknown figure's curiosity? Or was it because her pursuer already possessed whatever secrets the office might hold?

Laicos was flipping through the documents carefully, set out before him along with the three items Elathien had found in Magister Sirnos's office. The note in Irandis's hand, the cracked black gemstone, the red-black crystal. All the pieces of the puzzle.

"The Authority Arcane should have been notified the moment these pieces came to your attention." The investigator's voice carried a real anger this time.

"This is about the girl Irandis, and the Authority mages wouldn't care. They would have taken Blackheath apart in their focus on the relics, and fate take the truth. When we find that truth, we can call them in to deal with Sirnos's magic, but not before."

"You presume a great deal," Laicos said as he turned his attention to the files.

"An investigator treats all evidence with an impartial eye," Elathien said as she watched him, "weighing each piece separate and in total. For the patterns in the connections define a path to importance."

"Your quoting Bellas at me was tiresome the first time."

"Then start listening. You reject the connection between these murders and the death of Irandis not for the weight of evidence, but because I'm the one weighing it for you. You dislike me, and so you discount what I see."

"And what exactly do you see?" the young investigator asked coldly. Elathien noted that he didn't bother denying the accusation.

"It's what I don't see that catches my attention." Elathien fanned out the notes and loose pages like she might be shuffling cards in a riverside tavern. All the reports were in Dacani's hand, and represented a litany of the details of staffing and corrections at the refuge. "Infractions against institutional codes," she pointed out. "Violations of protocol, records of unexpected confrontation with violent convalescents." All of it was there, carefully recorded as single-page notes, then transcribed to a running ledger month by month. That ledger was open now to a date Elathien knew Laicos wouldn't recognize.

"That's the night Irandis died. There's the record of the death. There's the cross-reference to the statement by the sentry who found her body. References to the case number of the Guard, notwithstanding how the Guard did nothing when they were called in. But there's no record of notice or reprimand for the sentry who left the doors to the Laboratory Tower unlocked. No record that Lady Dacani even tried to find out which of the six sentries on duty that night it might have been. She added two more pages to the refuge's security protocols the week after Irandis died. But for the gross error of protocol causing the death of a convalescent, no reaction."

Laicos pushed the files away. "The absence of evidence isn't enough to point to conspiracy," the investigator said, dismissive. "A single expectation unfulfilled doesn't create a pattern."

"That's your pride talking," Elathien said, and as she did, she was reminded uncomfortably of having been on the other side of too many similar conversations as a young investigator of the Guard. "Telling you that if you can't solve the mystery on your own, it doesn't matter whether it gets solved. But it does matter. It matters to Nerani, it matters to your superiors, who will have questions for you when a copy of my report-for-hire to Blackheath arrives in the Tower of Law and points out the evidence you turned a blind eye to."

In Laicos's gaze as he stood, Elathien saw a sudden spike of anger that might have killed if the investigator possessed any strength of magic to back it up. He said nothing, though.

"It matters to Cirhela," Elathien added, "which means it matters to me, which means it matters to you."

"I think this obsession with the dead girl has far more to do with you than with Master Cirhela."

"You can think what you like."

"What I think is the truth. Because I know what this place is to you."

Elathien felt a faint tremor twist through her hands. She squeezed them shut. She heard the calculated tone in the investigator's voice, trying to judge how much of a bluff might stand behind it.

"You were an inmate here," he said. Not bluffing. "In the aftermath of the unfortunate business that saw you discharged from the Yewnyr Guard in disgrace."

Elathien covered her silence by scooping up the crystal, the gemstone, the note, slipping each one to a pocket of her belt. Her dismissal and the criminal record that came with it would have been an easy thing for Laicos to uncover. His contempt from that morning, his dismissiveness, had made good use of whatever he'd learned through his contacts at the Guard.

But what had happened afterward, the events that led Elathien to Blackheath, were things hidden beneath several layers of obfuscation. Some of those layers were her family's effort. Some were screens and diversions of her own making.

"And my being here taught me things you'll never understand," she said. She tried to find a coldness in her voice to match that in Laicos, but it was lost beneath an edge of emotion that she couldn't hide. "We're all broken. People like you, twisted in obvious ways. People better at hiding it. People who are forced to face it, like me."

Laicos offered up a smirk. "And so you become a crusader for the broken, finding them everywhere. Seeing reflections of yourself that you can pretend to fix like you can't fix the essential weakness in your own spirit."

"I see things I believe in, and I see the rest of the world telling me those things aren't important. The truth. Justice."

"The words of children, suitable for a girl playing in the world of men. Opportunistic as all women, and paying the price for her avarice. You betrayed your place in the Guard. You betrayed your rank."

"I was set up," Elathien hissed. She tried to force the anger into her voice now, but all she could feel instead was an old fear, threatening to break open inside her. "I was cut down by people with power, as you already know because you've read my records."

"I know the story your family paid to have planted in your records," Laicos laughed. "After you betrayed them, as well. The noble's daughter, Elathien of House Solorilthae. Disowned and disinherited, your brother…"

"My family's corruption is no business of yours." The tremor in Elathien's hands was in her voice now. "Even if it had anything to do with the truth…"

"I can read between the lines to find the truth. Weighing each piece of evidence separately and in total, recognizing that whatever madness you carried then is what brought you to Blackheath. And I suspect you carry it still."

Laicos stepped toward her, and then the two of them were circling around the desk and each other suddenly, Elathien unable to make herself stand firm.

"This place taught me what's important, and that you don't draw a line between right and wrong, between sense and madness based on what the majority insists is true…"

"I think you learned the arts of manipulating people long before you got here. This place only made you better at it, culminating in enticing Master Cirhela into a forbidden affair…"

"All of which happened after I was gone from here…"

"…not caring about her reputation, not caring about anyone except yourself. Taking advantage of the healer's weaknesses to pretend she was a person who could love someone as broken as you."

Elathien sent a backhand blow to the investigator's face with no warning, but Laicos was faster than he looked. He stopped her hand with his, surprising her for the first time since they'd met two days before.

Then he struck her in return. It was a weak blow, made weaker as she rolled back and away from it. A reaction mostly of surprise on his part, building on his anger, not enough to hurt her. A thing someone does when they feel control slipping, and everything she sensed in Laicos, everything he had just said to her, told Elathien how very much he liked to be in control.

She let her cloak drop, the tunic of black leather pulled over her head before Laicos had any sense of what she was doing. The white shift came with it, Elathien's skin pale in the bright light of the office's evenlamps. Old scars on her back and shoulders showed where the tattoos plunged down.

She grasped his hands and felt the muscle of his arms turned to water. Pulling him close, she forced him to cup her breasts, her pale nipples hardening as she pressed against and kissed him. She felt his uncertainty, felt his aversion, felt his sudden hunger overriding everything else. His control slipping, just as she wanted it.

She dropped to her knees before him, head bowed as if in supplication. Not watching his expression but feeling him react as she pressed her hands to his crotch, felt him already growing for her.

Even as he succumbed to the sudden spike of desire that Elathien drew from him, Laicos stayed as fully dressed as his excitement allowed, fumbling his trousers down just enough to free his hardness. Elathien took advantage of that to strip completely, peeling off her boots and her leather leggings. Her nakedness heightened the difference in their size, showing off the lean spareness of her body as he crushed her to him, forcing his tongue past hers with a groan.

All his anger was focused in the act as he dropped her to the office floor, rolling her to her knees and mounting her. Her legs were splayed as he held her down. As his sex found her wetness, his hand found the back of her neck, pinning her as she arched herself to meet him.

Elathien felt a much-needed thrill in reaction to his dominance, all because she knew how falsely fragile that dominance was. Despite the advantage of his height and weight, she instinctively counted five different ways she could have rolled him over with no effort. Three of those ways were likely to leave visible damage. One would have done its damage even before she turned him, and that damage would be long lasting and most personal.

But through the rough and rising pleasure of his hardness inside her, she let herself revel in the feel of granting him this false control, just for a little while. The sensation she felt now of giving herself over to another was a dangerous thrill for her, burning in her mind as strongly as the thrill of the suddenness of the tryst. She reveled in that suddenness, in the risk of exposure, even with Diranta on the other side of the door.

She felt a dark pain at the realization of which of Laicos's words had cut her the most.

Who could love someone as broken as you…

She remembered the feeling of Cirhela's tongue and fingers inside her two nights before. She remembered the grey spring morning nine months past, when she had left Cirhela's flat for what should have been the last time. She remembered the night before that grey morning, which had been the last time Cirhela told Elathien she loved her.

As she carried herself to the peak of pleasure a first time, Elathien employed the least risky of potential maneuvers to roll them both over. Laicos's expression underlined his surprise at being so easily toppled, Elathien riding him first back to front, then spinning around to face him, high and on her haunches. Now she was the one who pinned him down, both hands locked to his stones in a way that would crush them in a heartbeat if he tried to raise his arms against her.

He didn't. Merely tensed in sudden panic as he arched his belly against hers, his hardness filling her as he gasped in sweet pain and she closed her eyes. She thought of Cirhela again, and of other faces long-lost from her life.

Elathien climaxed a second time even as Laicos finished loudly. She released him to lean back, not surprised as he quickly pulled himself from her with a grimace.

"Brief and to the point," she said as she lay back on cold flag-stones, letting her breathing slow.

"And what was that point?" The unaccustomed doubt in the investigator's voice was exactly what she wanted.

"I'm mad," she said with a thin smile. "Hadn't you heard?"

Laicos was a type that she had spent her whole life facing off against. One who enjoyed the feel of control too much, Elathien thought, even as she reminded herself that she was no better than him in the moment. Taking almost as much pleasure in his discomfort as in the act just completed. Different forms of control.

"This changes nothing." Laicos had his back to her as he laced his leggings.

"You have an awfully high opinion of yourself if you can pretend it had any chance to."

"Then I ask again, what was the point?"

Elathien collected her clothing but waited until Laicos turned back to her before she began to dress. "Let's just say I needed to prove something," she said as she cleaned herself with her headscarf. She left it in Lady Dacani's wastebasket when she was done.

"And were you successful?"

"Yes," she lied as she pulled her shift on. And as she did, she tried in vain to push the memory of Cirhela, of the feel of the healer's body locked to hers, from her mind.

"Look after her," Elathien said as she pulled on her leggings and boots. "Cirhela. Tell her I'll be back in the morning."

"And where do you think you're going?"

"To inquire after some information I was on my way to seek out before Lady Dacani's untimely passing and our memorable evening together." She slipped the leather tunic on, careful to phrase her directives to Laicos in a way that would sound least like an order. "You should go over the records here, make sure I didn't miss anything. Then you'll need to interview the sentries and the sergeant at arms. Get confirmation that it was Tajamynar who left the doors open that led Irandis to her death that night. If they won't talk, threaten truth-magic and seize the sentry logs."

"My more immediate concern is the death here tonight. And the question of whether there'll be another. You talk like the killer is still at large in the refuge."

There was no indifference in the investigator's tone this time. Elathien felt the wetness that was the price of his conciliation on her thighs as she pulled her cloak across her shoulders and strode for the door. A bargain struck, she thought, as easy as that. Too easy, sometimes.

"Possibly. But another murder tonight doesn't fit the pattern. Different deaths, different days. Whoever's done this has moved freely, unseen. Sirnos, Tajamynar, and Dacani could have all been targeted with infinite swiftness if that was the intent. The fact that they weren't suggests the killer wanted each person in the chain to have time to be afraid."

"So you think there's another intended victim?"

"I don't know." Elathien turned back as she opened the door. Diranta looked up to see her, tail thumping the stone floor to tell her nothing was amiss. "But three victims with a connection to Irandis suggests that she's the place where it all starts. If we can find out who she was before she was lost, we might find out why she was lost. And what happened to her before the end."

— THIRTEEN —

THE JOURNEY COVERED more than half the city, crossing along the fringes of two dozen wards and passing uncounted twisting streets from Blackheath in Mirayth to Anduras Hamlets across the river. The clear night was cold with a wind from the northwest, so that Elathien hailed a hansom for its relative warmth.

My mother lived in refuge, at the great house of Maera the Huntress. My father died in the work gangs, six years after I was born... Not a lot of information to go on, but it was less than Elathien often started with.

The fanes of the old gods of Gracia could be found in almost every ward these days. When Elathien was a child, she had scoffed at her grandfather's tales of a Free City under Empire two generations before, its people and culture free of the dead faiths of the past. But those dead faiths had been coming back to life since before Elathien was born, starting first and establishing themselves most strongly among the wards of the better-off working classes. Anduras Hamlets was chief of these, a broad expanse of apartments and houses, shops and guildhalls in the shadow of the Ridge, toward which many of the ward's residents looked with dark aspiration.

She found the temple of Maera without difficulty, the cab driver confirming that although smaller temples to the Huntress were scattered throughout the ward, there was no other refuge save the temple the locals called the great house. She told the driver to run two streets beyond, then walked back. Old habits, she thought as she pulled her cloak tight around her against the cold.

Where they took on the role of refuges for the indigent and the sick, the temples of Yewnyr were much like Blackheath in their own way. But like all the gods' houses, the holy refuges were driven by the piety of creed and the teachings of the priests, rather than by the will of folk to simply aid each other for the simple sake of caring. Elathien had little patience for the struggles of faith, but the faith of self that had been the faith of Empire seemed a good enough way to live. The idea of helping others only by way of mystic compulsion felt like a small thing, somehow.

The night was bitter, smoke rising in thin columns to shroud the stars. She crossed the street between staggered coach traffic and a single rickshaw, its shirtless Dwarven runner blithely showing his indifference to the weather. She watched the street closely as she approached, though she knew there was nothing to fear here. Old habits.

At the temple's dark doors, she rapped a knocker of freezing brass with a hand wrapped in her cloak. She waited only a short while before the doors cracked open to a robed figure, an oil lamp held high.

"My name is Elathien," she said, "a sanctioned investigator on liaison to the Yewnyr Guard." She raised the wallet with her investigator's credentials into the light in one hand. With the other, she showed Laicos's badge, which she had lifted without notice from his cloak as she rode him. "I seek entrance to the refuge and answers to questions regarding folk who might have dwelled or worked here fifteen years ago. I won't trouble you long."

The silent doorkeeper appraised both sets of credentials before fitting a great steel key to the lock. He pulled the gate shut behind Elathien as she slipped inside.

The courtyard was dark, frost on the cobbles gleaming faintly where the Clearmoon swelled and swirled beyond the clouds. The walls of the temple rose to a faintly oppressive gloom above, a scattering of windows bright with light. The ground-floor apartment where the doorkeeper led Elathien was likewise well lit, with a white-coal fire in the sitting room burning against the chill. The doorkeeper slipped farther inside while Elathien waited, pacing carefully as she motioned for Diranta to stay by the door.

It was an elderly priest who returned a short while later, nodding to Elathien and making some kind of sign she didn't bother to return. No risk of insulting him that way, she thought, the rituals of piety a thing she had never spent any real time worrying about.

"Call me Irasa," the priest intoned as he motioned her to sit. "What is it you seek?" At a sideboard, he poured brandy in elegant goblets of blown glass. "I mean no disrespect to the law or your person, but I'll not wake the high priest of the house without cause."

"Only information," Elathien said. "Questions of the past." She nodded thanks for the brandy as he handed it to her, the light of the room's lamps shimmering in the goblet's golden depths. "Have you worked here long, might I ask?"

"All my life, for what it is. Twenty-eight summers past it was that I came to serve the Huntress, just after the old High Priest Ilseus had gone to his reward at Maera's side."

"Then you might know of a woman who once lived here in refuge. I don't know her name, but I was told she gave birth to daughters at this place. Irandis and Nerani."

A look of surprise and the hint of a smile came over the old man, but an edge of suspicion kept it from transforming the wariness of his expression.

"By my faith and fate," he said. "That was Salina, to be sure. But there wouldn't be more than a dozen people who would know those two girls' names, and all of those should know their mother's name as well."

"I offer apologies for my ignorance, but I'm afraid I've entered their story only recently. You said 'that was Salina.' Is she dead, then?"

"Aye, mistress. She died in the birth of the girls, I'm afraid, or short afterward. And a dark night that was to be sure, with a storm wind beyond the walls that screamed as if seeking vengeance on the city itself."

"So the girls were born here?"

"Aye, and both were bright treasures to be sure. But Salina hadn't believed in the healers, you see. One of the Kelist, she was, so respectful of the Huntress's ways, but putting faith only in the magic of her folk's tree-priests. Wouldn't hold with the healing of any other, and more than she paid for it in the end. The midwife did what she could, but Salina was weak from bleeding."

The old man's voice was a dull echo against the dark-paneled walls. Elathien sipped at her brandy, hearing the heaviness of memory in his words and not wanting to push him. But her own mood was on edge as a result of the atmosphere around her. An oppressive air of wealth and secrecy. Too much of a sense of familiarity with her own childhood, she thought. The temples of the old gods, the apartments of the nobility, all oiled wood and dark rituals. Too much a sense of ready-made reverence for her taste.

"After Salina passed, another of the women here, Irmata her name was, served as wet-nurse. A three-month-old at her breast already, and everyone doing what we could in our goddess Maera's name, and with the blessings of all the priests to be sure. But then young Irandis was claimed by her father. A waterfront bravo by his reputation, and an unscrupulous sort he always looked to me. Four summers she might have been, the girl already whip smart for her age. She didn't want to go, and Irmata didn't want to give her up, but he had the law on his side and nothing to do about it."

"He took Irandis but not Nerani? Why?"

The priest's look changed to sudden puzzlement. "Wee Nerani died, mistress."

An ice-water chill twisted down the length of Elathien's spine. She stared into the golden light of her goblet for a long moment, her thoughts suddenly thick in her head, twisting like fog.

"I'm sorry. What did you say?"

"Nerani was the wee one, mistress. Weak from waiting for her sister to be born, the midwife said. She died in her mother's arms just a heartbeat after she named her, and two heartbeats before Salina herself passed."

"Nerani…" Elathien wrapped her other hand around the goblet where it was trembling. "Nerani died. Irandis lived."

"Aye. Nerani and her mother both are buried in Sarys Green, out on the Thirty League Way."

It wasn't what she had expected.

Of all the things it could have been, of all the things she could have learned here this night, Elathien had never so much as speculated on the possibilities and the understanding that spilled open around her now. She felt the darkness press down harder, Diranta sensing the fear in her as he rose against her earlier command, coming close to nuzzle her leg.

"Are you all right, mistress?"

She focused to see the priest watching her, concerned now. She nodded as she forced a thin smile.

"I'm just sorry to be the bearer of bad news. Irandis was friend to a friend of mine, who wanted me to let you know that she had died."

The pain in the priest's suddenly frowning gaze was tangible. All those years lost, and a memory of a girl four summers old could still cut him this way. "That's a sad thing, make no mistake. So young, still."

"Yes," Elathien said. "So young." The goblet found her lips and she drained it in one pull. The priest followed suit, taking it for a toast.

"To Irandis, then. She had a good life I trust? To have friends who would come all this way with such news, I mean?"

"Yes," Elathien lied. "A good life."

"I often wondered how much the lass would even remember of this place. She was so young."

"She remembered it all." Elathien heard herself speak the words as if from some great distance. "She remembered Nerani even. Right to the end..."

She was running, fighting to breathe in the chill air. She felt her hasty departure from the temple as a faint blur in her mind, not thinking about what she said as she made her excuses to the priest. Not thinking how she had slipped out the great black doors and broken into a run.

Diranta was at her side as she finally slowed, pacing around her as if he sensed her fear but couldn't tell its source. She saw cabs and coaches flash past on the adjacent streets, but there was no point in shouting for one. Blackheath was half the city away, and she had no time anymore.

From her cloak, Elathien fumbled the steel talisman. Its runes were gleaming with a pale light like they hadn't before, as if they sensed her need. She felt the relic's teleportation magic, familiar to her from her previous study, but still not giving her any sense of how to use the piece. She wasn't sure if it even had the range to return her to Blackheath, or of what might happen if her attempt to call on its power failed. An errant teleport could kill, she knew.

She knelt to the ground, grabbing Diranta in her arms and holding tight. She closed her eyes, visualizing the place in Blackheath that she knew more intimately than any other. Cirhela's offices, where so many long days of pain and hope had been spent. Her first real memories of the refuge had been those high windows, the walls with their paintings of sunlight and green fields. Cirhela's voice, telling her who she was, what had happened to her. Promising that she could make it better.

Elathien focused her mind on that voice, on those windows and walls. She felt an unfamiliar lurch as the chill wind and noise of the street were suddenly replaced with a pulse of warmth and silence, interrupted by a shout of alarm that filtered in as if from a distance. Diranta was growling in her arms, fighting her in a way he never did as he flailed away from her, dropping low to the floor. His teeth were bared in reaction to the unfamiliar threat of the transition, but a glance around her told Elathien that the talisman had worked.

She stood shakily in Cirhela's offices, under the gaze of Laicos and two other members of the Guard where they were carefully going through the master healer's files. She wasn't sure which of the guards had cried out, but she saw Laicos thankfully holding them off from any action with a wave of his hand.

"I assume that asking for an explanation would be a waste of my time?"

"I need to speak to Cirhela," Elathien said by way of affirmation. "And you, alone. I know what's happening."

"I'd like to speak to Cirhela myself," Laicos said darkly. "We've been looking for her since you left."

Elathien stepped to Diranta where he was still growling, kneeling to calm him. She couldn't focus her thoughts, but whether that was from some lingering effect of the magic that brought her here or from the truth she had learned, she didn't know. Her hand was shaking as she slipped the talisman back to the pocket of her cloak.

"Did she return home? Is she safe?"

"A runner sent to her residence came back with no word of her. We have watchers on her door in case she returns. Unless you know where else she might be?"

Elathien felt a chill twist through her. She stood, pacing across to Laicos. "She was with one of your guards. He walked her away from the garden. I told you."

The look on Laicos's face told her the investigator had forgotten that conversation in the heat of what had come after.

"None of my guards have seen her," he said. "She's left the refuge, or she's hiding here, and either way, I'm forced to wonder why." His tone was dark as he turned away. Elathien grabbed him by the shoulder, spinning him back with a strength that elicited a look of surprise.

In her mind, she pulled back the fleeting memory. She saw Cirhela at the edge of the crowd gathering in the corridors beyond the garden. She saw the healer's gaze flick back once, fear on her face. She watched the guard's retreating back, the black and red cloak coming up around Cirhela's shoulder.

In a sudden flash of certainty, she recognized the thickness of the arm that had raised that cloak. She was a fool.

"Close the building," she said as she broke from Laicos and headed for the door. "Seal all the entrances, look for an Essaruk in the uniform of the Guard but not in your command. No one gets in or out." Diranta was at her heel with a snap of her fingers. She didn't look back as she ran.

— FOURTEEN —

RACING ALONG the empty corridors of the Administration Tower for the nearest stairs, Elathien had to slow to pull the cracked black gemstone from her belt. She held it tight, feeling its arcane power open up to her. The stones of sending were common enough in the city, used by those whose business turned to secrets and espionage. Among the most common items of the black markets, their usefulness as a means of connecting two wielders, mind to mind and thought to thought, was also their greatest security.

If lost or separated, the stones were all but useless, granting no ability to track or trace back to the party on the other end of the link. One had to already know who the recipient was before the dweomer and connection within the cracked gem could be activated.

Elathien knew now who had always been at the other end of the stone in Magister Sirnos's desk.

"Cahlad!" she screamed in her mind. *"If Cirhela is harmed in any way, this ends with my knives in your heart."*

She felt the link surge in a way that told her the Essaruk enforcer was listening. The act of using the stones was an uncomfortable one for her, creating a sense of her mind being wide open. She had to fight that feeling, knowing that only the thoughts she focused down to a handful of words would be readable at the other end.

"Two fools in over your heads, Elf." Cahlad's voice in her head carried the same accent she had heard in the empty flat two nights before, a mocking quality twisting through it even as raw thought. *"One chance to see your lover alive. Find the girl. Come to where it happened. No guards."*

Elathien didn't bother answering, but she kept the stone at hand in case the Essaruk had any other words for her. He was looking for the girl. Nerani. Elathien felt herself shiver, having to force the name into her mind. This meant that Cahlad hadn't found her, even though he would have looked in all the places she should have been.

Elathien didn't know what that might mean.

She took the stairs two at a time, the corridors around her deserted as she crossed through the wards. At each locked door, she worked her picks with frantic speed, some kind of lockdown imposed in the aftermath of Lady Dacani's death, she guessed. No one to get in the way of what Elathien feared would happen here this night. She ran with a strength born of fear and a growing rage as she hit the stairs to the Laboratory Tower, that energy compensating in its own way for the spellpower that was all but exhausted in her. She felt for one final surge of arcane strength, holding it ready as she sprinted along the last corridor and kicked through the door. Already understanding that it wouldn't be enough.

The door cracked through its frame and slammed to strike the wall beyond. The evenlamps in the laboratory where Irandis died were shrouded, the blinds at the windows drawn so that the Clearmoon's light passed through only in razor-thin sheets. Like all his kind, the Essaruk was well at home in total darkness, Elathien knew. However, she was at no disadvantage even in the faint light, her Ilvani eyes pulling all detail from the shadows.

Cahlad was against the wall beneath the windows, the truncheons left at his belt in favor of a hunting knife he held to Cirhela's throat. He was stripped to the waist for combat, the uniform of a Yewnyr Guard torn off and abandoned a few strides away. Dried blood at a gash on his forehead told Elathien that however he had gotten the drop on Cirhela after leading her away from the garden, it hadn't been easy for him.

The healer was bruised and gagged, her hands bound with leather thongs. Presumably, she had been in this state all the while that Elathien had traveled to Anduras Hamlets to seek the truth that was a tight knot in her gut now. Cirhela was struggling despite the threat of the blade, Elathien knowing that the healer was more than capable of stepping up even to a fight she had no chance of winning. It was what she was counting on as she unleashed the last of her magic at a run.

She snarled her incantation, and from the fingers of one outstretched hand, a blade of white light streaked out to unerringly strike the Essaruk full in the face.

Cahlad shouted out in pain as he staggered back. It was all the distraction Cirhela needed to twist, forcing his iron grip away as she dropped to the ground. Diranta was ahead of Elathien, snarling as he went for the Essaruk's leg to throw him further off balance. Finally, the dog was able to tag the scent he had followed through Blackheath twice before, recognizing the Essaruk from the encounter in Irandis's empty flat.

Elathien cursed herself for not realizing that sooner, willing all her own anger into Diranta's attack. But even through the distraction and the pain, Cahlad managed to lash out at Cirhela, Elathien seeing the haft of his blade catch the healer across the temple. Her head snapped back soundlessly as she collapsed to the floor.

Elathien was past her, vaulting from the table to unleash another bolt of arcane force at the snarling Essaruk. The last of her spellpower, spent over the past three frantic days, was gone. As the knife of white light left her fingers, her hands swung back and behind her, drawing both long-knives from their scabbards. She slashed twin arcs of steel as she hit, Diranta snarling as he came in with her.

Even as fast as Elathien was, even with the dog at her side and the fury that was the blood rage running through her, it wasn't enough.

Cahlad was a street fighter, rolling back from her attack as he drew one truncheon, then counterstruck with a speed that nearly took Elathien's head off. She twisted away and struck again, feeling the force behind her blades dulled by callused skin as strong as cured leather. She gauged the rhythm of the Essaruk's staggered assault, stepping through the blur of the nail-studded truncheon twice. But as she did, the knife in Cahlad's off hand slipped in to tag her at the hip.

A pain like white-hot fire tore through her leg as she stumbled back, both knives up to parry a follow-on strike. Except that follow-on strike twisted away from her faster than she could follow. Cahlad's truncheon struck down instead. Diranta cried out with a shrieking howl of pain as he was struck full force in the shoulder. Then the dog collapsed unmoving to the floor.

As Elathien backpedaled around the nearest table, she risked the moment that it took to glance to Cirhela still sprawled behind her. She had no idea whether Diranta was dead or alive, not enough time to see whether Cirhela was breathing, hot tears stinging her eyes. As Cahlad lunged toward her, she took advantage of her size, leaping up and over the table to circle around behind him. Two fast slashes and the Essaruk was stumbling back, howling in pain. She leaped forward for a fast follow-up.

Then she saw Cahlad smirk as he grasped at a gleam of steel at his belt. He carried a talisman to match the one in Elathien's pocket, the token of teleportation that had carried the Essaruk into the refuge and away from her twice that day.

Elathien tried to change her course, but momentum carried her, throwing her off balance as she struck at the empty air where Cahlad vanished. She wasn't fast enough to spin before he appeared two strides behind her, laying into her with both truncheons and sending her down.

The room twisted around her as the floor shimmered before her eyes like wind-blown cloud. Elathien could taste blood in her mouth, her right arm numb. The long-knife it once held had fallen four strides away. Cahlad was closer, strutting toward her with both truncheons crossed over his bare chest.

"Where is the girl?" the Essaruk roared. "I grow tired of orders not followed! Not in her rooms, not in the wards, not where the healer can find her. This ends tonight!"

From the corner of her eye, Elathien saw Cirhela move. Her eyes flicked open, staring with a focus that told Elathien she'd been awake for a while now. With effort, the healer twisted her hands free of the leather thongs where she had loosened them while Elathien fought. She tore the gag from her mouth, and even in the moment that it took Cahlad's attention to turn to her, Cirhela had summoned up magic of her own.

She clutched at the sigil of Blackheath at her shoulder, focusing her power as she shouted out the incantation of her spell. The faintest shadow streaked through the air between her and Cahlad, occluding the Essaruk in a fast-fading shimmer of force that froze him where he stood.

Elathien was conscious of a sudden pulse of sound that was her own breathing, telling her she must have blacked out for a moment. She was on the other side of the room, Cirhela's arms wrapped around her as the power of healing magic surged through her. She felt the pain at her leg and shoulder begin to unweave itself, the wounds not fully healed but closing at least. The dull ache that clouded her mind showed no sign of fading, however.

Cahlad was held at the perfect frozen apex of his threatened attack, but Elathien knew he wouldn't stay that way for long. They had to get out quickly, but as she tried to say so to Cirhela, something else came out.

"Nerani…" she whispered.

Cirhela followed Elathien's gaze to the doorway where Nerani stood. The girl was a thin shadow, the white of her robe catching the light of the corridor beyond. The healer rose, one arm still around Elathien to lift her as she called out.

"Nerani, you can't be here!"

"No," Elathien whispered. Her strength was returning but her voice was trapped in the fear that closed off her throat.

"You're in danger, Nerani," Cirhela said. "You need to come with us. Do you understand?"

"These things that had to happen…" The girl's voice was a steel-edged whisper, a sadness twisting through her words like Elathien had never heard, could never have imagined. She understood it, though. "There are threads running through these lives that cannot be cut."

Shakily, as if she knew of the end that was coming and hoped to avoid it even now, Nerani took a step toward Cahlad's frozen form.

Cirhela tried to break away, but Elathien locked her arms around her, let the dead weight of her own body hold her down. "Let me go," the healer hissed.

"There are so many things that I have forgotten," Nerani said. "So many things I wish I could see." She turned to level her cold gaze at Elathien, who felt the fear suddenly break beneath the weight of acceptance in those eyes. "You said you don't believe in vengeance. But when everything else is lost, sometimes vengeance is all that's left to you."

"But that doesn't make it right," Elathien said. "You being here, what you did to them. It won't bring her back." She felt Cirhela tense against her body, the healer with no way to understand.

"There is a place beyond right and wrong," Nerani whispered. "I've been there. Irandis is there now. I hope you never have to see it yourself."

With a sudden scream of fury, Cahlad was moving.

Cirhela's spell had been broken by the Essaruk's rage, and he used the momentum of his last movement toward Elathien to twist into position. Even as his body was held fast, his sight and thoughts had been as active as ever, so that he sized up Cirhela and Elathien immobile on the floor, swinging past them. In two bounds, he was on top of Nerani, spinning her as he twisted one rope-muscled arm across her chest, his knife in his other hand and pressed to her throat.

"A remarkable resemblance," he hissed. At the corner of his eye that had Nerani's profile in sight as he watched Elathien and Cirhela on the floor, he let the blade of the knife wander up along her chin, her cheek. For her part, Nerani made no sign of fear, her small body unnaturally relaxed in the Essaruk's vicelike grip. "A shame that this one did not turn up while her sister was alive. What a treat together they would have made."

Elathien couldn't focus. She wasn't ready for this, still waiting for her reflexes to return. She needed to stall for time, feeling her way around a thought that came suddenly to mind. Something she should have realized before, but her reaction to the knowledge of Irandis's life had thrown her. Too many things in that life that seemed to remind her of herself. A rookie mistake.

"Fourteen Lights," she said thickly. "Nerani spoke of 'a house of Fourteen Lights'. Not 'the house'. Because she knew there were others. Other children, locked up tight in other apartments, other wards. Slaves to the perversion that pays you to protect it."

Cahlad simply smiled, flashing the hideous grin of wide-spread canines.

"You destroyed her," Elathien said. "Irandis." She could feel her head clearing, could feel the taunting edge of her words undercutting the Essaruk's own focus. But at the same time, over and above the need to stall, she realized how badly she wanted to hear Cahlad admit the truth before the end. "The crystals that Sirnos used. Dark magic. It stole her mind, burned away her memories. Destroyed everything she was. You couldn't afford to kill her, because you feared that she might have already started to tell what she knew. Too many people whose reputations might suffer if her death was investigated. So you would make her appear insane instead. Discounting everything she knew as the ravings of a madwoman."

"Smart girl." The Essaruk smiled again. "Smart, but slow. So see if you are quicker this time. I have my own means of transport but have exhausted its magic. So you and the healer will escort the sister and I out past the Guard and sentries you have no doubt ordered to the doors, yes? Once we are outside, the healer accompanies us to Crad Road Gate by coach cab. Outside the walls, away from the Guard, they are both set free. Quick and easy, yes?"

"The place you're going, you won't need transport, Cahlad..."

Elathien felt her breath leave her suddenly, a sharp pain twisting in her side. Cirhela had taken advantage of the distraction of Elathien's anger to elbow her hard in the ribs, breaking her grip. The healer shot to her feet, calling Nerani's name before Elathien heard her begin the incantation to another spell.

"Stay away!" It took all Elathien's effort to whip herself around, striking Cirhela full force in the right knee. She heard something in the healer's leg crack as she came crashing down, her spell lost.

"I can stop him!" Cirhela shouted, pain twisting through her voice. Even injured, she was pulling away from Elathien, hitting hard to break her grip. "I won't let him…"

"No!" Elathien shouted, pulling Cirhela back with still-failing strength. "You need to stay away from her!"

From nowhere, a wind began to rise.

The murderous light in Cahlad's eyes darkened then. Just for a moment, as if he heard the warning for Cirhela in Elathien's voice and understood what it meant.

In his arms, Nerani hadn't moved. She stood limp, like Cahlad's arm might be the only thing holding her up. But she raised one hand suddenly, touching her fingers to the Essaruk's knife hand. And as Elathien watched, that hand ruptured like a grey leather sack of blood and bone.

Cahlad screamed. The knife fell. A gout of foul effluent showered Nerani, but the girl made no sign that she felt it. The Essaruk staggered back from her, pain breaking his grip, but Nerani turned to face him, raising her hand in a sweeping motion that seemed to stop him dead. He was held fast in the manner of the spellpower that Cirhela had used on him. But unlike the effect of that spell, Nerani's power left him shaking, snarling in fear and pain.

"How many times did you have her, beast?" Nerani's voice was barely a whisper, but the storm held within that voice shrieked and howled around her. Cahlad tried to scream in response, but his throat was full of blood suddenly, choked up past the snarling fangs and the ashen grey lips. "How many times did she pay the price of your animal passion? The times you beat her, raped her, subjected her to your degradation in the name of breaking her. To make her the puppet your masters needed her to be."

Elathien didn't need to present the cantrip of detection to feel the magical power that surged in Nerani now. A power that hadn't been in her any of the times she had spoken to the girl. A power that had no precedent. The wind was like something ethereal, twisting through her even though she couldn't feel it. The touch of a memory, chilling her to the bone.

"Irandis called to me." Nerani whispered her dead sister's name like a benediction. "She called me back from the place I waited for her. And then I was here, carrying her pain to return it whence it came."

Cahlad fell to his knees, bleeding now from eyes and ears. He was convulsing, his body writhing like the storm wind was scouring him from within. Nerani turned back to face Elathien's wide-eyed gaze, Cirhela staring in stark fear.

"Thank you," she said to both of them. "For caring." Her voice was the sound of the howling gale that Elathien realized suddenly was the first and only thing the infant Nerani would have heard in her too-short life. *A dark night,* the priest had said, *with a storm wind beyond the walls that screamed as if seeking vengeance...*

A sadness threaded through the girl, echoing the pain in her very young eyes. Then she closed those eyes, and the tall windows of the laboratory exploded inward in a rain of lead fragments and shattered glass.

Cirhela cried out as Elathien drew her down beneath her, turning her own back to the deadly storm of shards. But that storm passed over and around them, focusing in on Cahlad as he screamed. From the corner of her eye, Elathien could see Diranta, also untouched where he was sprawled across the room from her. Because she couldn't watch, because she had to make herself look away, she focused on the dog, feeling something stirring in her when she thought she saw his chest rise and fall, just once.

Then all was silent, and it was done.

Cahlad's skin had been flensed from his body in jagged strips, laid down like some hunter's trophy pelt atop the cloud of red-black effluent that stained the floor. His weapons, his clothing, even the talisman of teleportation at his waist had been shattered down to shards, slowly sinking now into the gore.

Cirhela was still in Elathien's arms, choking as she turned away. Elathien held the healer's head tight to her breast, blocking the view as she stumblingly walked her to the door. She was too numb to be surprised as she saw Laicos there, breathless like he had been running in an attempt to discover where Elathien had gone. The look on his face told her he had seen the end.

She left Cirhela with him. The crunch of glass and splintered bone was loud under her boots as she returned for Diranta, lifting him carefully. He was breathing, but roughly, his coat soaked through with blood from his shattered shoulder. Cirhela numbly summoned up a spell of healing for the dog as Elathien turned back to the laboratory one last time.

No tracks traced through the gore of the room except for Elathien and Cirhela's. Angling low to the corridor floor, she could see the faint marks of bare footprints on the tiles where they had approached the laboratory door.

No matching tracks went back in the opposite direction, though. Nerani was gone.

— FIFTEEN —

THE HAZE OF SUNLIT SKY was bright above the garden, the chill of winter air softened further by the shroud of magic that cloaked the stones and trees. Elathien had her cloak off, letting the dark leather of her tunic and leggings draw in the warmth. Only midmorning after the night Lady Dacani died, the signs of her grim end a dozen paces from where Elathien sat had been meticulously cleaned away. As would be expected, however, the garden was conspicuously empty, Elathien and Diranta seeing no one else all morning.

The dog was sprawled along the magic-warmed flagstones at her feet, happily sleeping the day away. Elathien hadn't slept yet, but the strange surge of life that seemed always to come from having seen death up close was carrying her nicely. After Cirhela's healing, both she and Diranta were none the worse for the near-fatal wounds they had taken. A jagged black scar at the dog's shoulder marked where the truncheon's spikes had punched through, but it would be less notice-able by spring when Elathien clipped his hair shorter.

She was absently stroking Diranta's belly with the toe of her boot when she saw him lift his head, so that she knew someone was coming.

"I'm sorry," Cirhela called. "I've been… dealing with things."

"You're master healer and head administrator," Elathien said without looking. "You should get used to it."

"Acting head administrator. Someone will replace Lady Dacani in time."

"Whoever it is will inherit the task of dealing with her deception and Magister Sirnos's. I'd be willing to bet that the Council of Masters will conveniently leave you with the job until the mess is dealt with."

"Perhaps." Cirhela shrugged as she sat. She leaned close to rub Diranta's ears, neither woman speaking for a time.

"So what are you going to do to weather the storm?" Elathien said at last.

"Focus on the good that comes to the refuge's reputation as a re-sult of the proper analysis and understanding of what happened here."

"And do you know what that is yet? The dead returning to the world, but not as undead?"

"A creature resurrected to life and restored to time by the sheer power of spite and vengeance. A magical phenomenon outside the scope of anything yet recorded, outside of even legend. Some on the council are saying we need to take stronger measures against another event."

"Irandis is dead. Nerani is gone. I think it's safe to say it's over."

"You're talking like what happened can be analyzed in terms of the mundane world."

"Vengeance is the most mundane thing in the world," Elathien said quietly. And then because she heard a question she didn't want to answer forming on Cirhela's lips, she changed the subject. "Laicos's people are back from Anduras Hamlets?"

"Yes. With statements sworn under truth magic, though we didn't need it. The priest Irasa made no lie. Nerani died as a babe."

"And fifteen years later, came back to the world," Elathien said, and the edge of fear that threaded her voice surprised her still. All the things she had seen in her life, all the wonders of a world built on the power of magic, and the unknown secrets of that magic were sometimes too terrible to know.

"Something's troubling you…"

More than one thing, Elathien thought. But she knew that by focusing on one of those things, she would be able to push the others away. Eventually.

"Irandis didn't run when she had the chance." It was a thing that had been bothering her since that afternoon in the records room, when she had assessed the dweomer in the steel talisman that hung beneath her tunic now. "Cahlad and his important people would have been too important to be seen going to the flat. The talismans were their way in and out. She had one hidden, must have stolen it at some point. She had the magic that would have let her flee at any time, gone to any safe place she knew."

"Perhaps because for her, there were no safe places anymore," Cirhela said. "But her keeping the talisman shows that she hadn't given up yet. She was waiting for a time when she could use it."

Elathien felt a double layer of meaning in the healer's words. She tried to give Diranta the signal to rise, looking for an excuse to do so herself, but he ignored her in favor of Cirhela's hand stroking his side.

"Sometimes," Cirhela said, "it's not enough to see the door. You need to have someone waiting on the other side."

"I should go." Elathien stood even without the excuse, kicking Diranta softly to get him to his feet. He did so, though he didn't look happy about it. "I was just waiting because I wanted to say goodbye. I'm sure you're busy."

"I am." Cirhela stood with Elathien, smoothing her robe. "So busy, in fact, that I was thinking the task might go easier with assistance. Whatever Dacani and Sirnos did here, I'm worried that they might have had arrangements with others like Cahlad. It'll be well hidden, though. Blackheath could use a full-time investigator, at least for a while. If you'd like to stay."

"I would like to, actually." The lie. "But I can't." The truth. And what bothered Elathien most was how difficult it was to feel the difference between truth and lie anymore.

"What happened to us?" Cirhela said quietly. It was a question that Elathien had been avoiding for nine months now. A question she had known she would have to answer someday, even as she left Cirhela's flat back on that grey spring morning.

"What happened to us was a wonderful accident." The edge of an unexpected honesty broke in Elathien's voice. "The things that brought us together were things I couldn't understand or name. But I can't live my life not knowing my life, and when I tried to figure out what we were, I broke what we were."

"Magic is uncontrollable." Cirhela echoed Elathien's own words back at her, seemingly from much farther away than only the night before. "So it's easy to assume it has no causality. Love is the same way, I think you'll find."

Elathien said nothing in response.

Cirhela hugged her as if she knew it was the last time. She made to turn away but Elathien held her back to kiss her, because she knew it was the last time. Then they walked from the garden together, Cirhela heading for the Masters' Tower as Elathien turned for the stairs without a word.

The unseen sun had turned the sky to a summer-bright sheen of blue above the rooftops, but the street before Blackheath was cold. Having passed the main gates, Elathien slung her cloak on, walking quickly with Diranta at her heel. The wind had picked up, but a hint of early spring had come with it. Elathien was ready for it.

She was walking past the tavern patio from which she had watched the traffic before Blackheath that morning three days before. The place where she had waited and watched for Laicos even before knowing him, so that it seemed almost appropriate to catch a glimpse of him at the same patio now. Waiting and watching for her.

She didn't approach him, but she felt him rise and fall into step behind her, then beside her. The street was crowded, but those crowds knowingly parted around them both as they noted the Guard cloak and the insignia at his shoulder.

"Good morning," he said.

Elathien didn't meet his gaze as she handed back the badge of rank she had stolen from him the night before. "So far."

Laicos quickly slipped it away within his cloak. "Assuming that your business at Blackheath is done, I wanted to thank you for your assistance. And to apologize for… my actions last night."

"Nonsense." Elathien reached over to squeeze his crotch, in plain view of every person walking toward them. "You weren't that bad."

Laicos furled his cloak in front of him as he gently batted her hand away. "I meant for my words. Before."

"Everything you said was true, and none of it matters anymore. Nothing could possibly require less apology." Even as she spoke, though, Elathien was gauging the uncertainty in the investigator's own voice. Where she glanced up to him, the expression on his face was one familiar to her.

He caught her gaze, recognizing the moment he'd been waiting for. "I would like to see you again. Professionally. And personally."

Elathien laughed. "Perhaps, and no, and you have no idea how much this is the wrong day to ask that."

Laicos simply nodded. "Then thank you again." But even as he shifted away from her, Elathien reached for his hand, pulling him close.

"The Fourteen Lights needs to be taken down and its backers broken," she said, "and I'm sure you'll be asked to take a lead role in light of this case exposing them." She gave him a sidelong glance. "But Blackheath also requires a full-time investigator. Master Cirhela needs assistance to discover the full scope of what Magister Sirnos and the others were up to, and you'll likely find more clues to the Fourteen Lights there than you will in the city. Whoever's behind the militia will already be going to ground. You should ask for short leave from the Guard and offer Cirhela your services. You'll do well."

Diranta came up between them both to nuzzle Elathien's hand where it held Laicos's. She smiled as she disengaged, noting the resistance in the investigator's fingers as she did.

"Why do you say that?" he asked, uncertain. "I mean, I thank you. But if you don't mind my asking, why has your opinion of me changed?"

"Because you know some things now that you didn't know before. Which means that from here on in, you'll always remember how much you don't know. That's the first axiom of the investigator's art." It wasn't Bellas, but something she had learned herself. It had served her well so far.

Elathien stopped short, Laicos halting a step beyond her. She appraised him with an investigator's eye. Even with her in boots, she realized that he was taller than she'd noticed before. She liked that.

"I need to sleep," she said, "as do you by the look of it. Ahlgarb House, Eburaci Lane in Kardonhill. Left at the Broken Archer and up the stairs. Be there after dusk tonight."

Laicos's surprise was genuine. She saw him forced to hide a smile. "But you said no…"

"I said no to seeing you personally. I promise you'll enjoy this, but it won't be personal."

Then she turned away and into the flow of traffic, sprinting to hop up to an empty rickshaw passing at full speed. Diranta raced alongside, waiting for Elathien to shift over so he could leap to the seat beside her. The runner was a grinning Dwarf whose legs were as thick around as Elathien's waist.

"You got a destination in mind, mistress?" he shouted back to her as she settled in.

Diranta was leaning over the edge, tongue lolling and tail wagging. Elathien looked back once to see Laicos striding after her, people to the sides clearing the way for his investigator's uniform as he kept her in sight for as long as he could.

"I want to sleep," she called, "with the wind blowing and the city shouting and the sun on my face. Keep to any streets that can give me that, and you can take me wherever you want."

COLOPHON

In addition to the authors thanking each other,
their gratitude is bestowed upon the following.
First round at the Broken Archer is on us.

The Feeling of Having Come Home
The families Hamilton and Craig/Gray

In the Records Room
Colleen Craig, Mitchell Wylie, Gabriel Duclair

Still Lifes in Watercolor
(studio)Effigy, Angela Hawkey

Sentries and Healers
Blue October, Jacqueline Carey, Dead Can Dance, John Debney,
Evanescence, Gary Gygax, Tami Hoag, Ty Johnston,
Colin McComb, James Patterson, Edgar Alan Poe

BLACKHEATH

AN ELATHIEN SOLO MYSTERY
·
A Novel of the Endlands

Published by Insane Angel Studios
insaneangel.com

Cover Design and Typography by (studio)Effigy
Elathien by Angela Hawkey

ISBN 978-1-927348-24-6

v1.0
September 2012

We try to make sure that no errors creep into our work, but publishing is a chaotic enterprise at the best of times. If you spot a typo or a formatting glitch in an Insane Angel Studios book, email insaneangel@insaneangel.com with details (including which e-book version you're reading, if applicable). If any errors you spot are ones we haven't yet caught and are in the process of fixing, you'll receive one of our e-books of your choice for free.